BLACKBEARD, TERROR OF THE SEAS

by Jean Day

Illustrated by Douglas W. Campbell

Golden Age Press
Newport NC 28570

BLACKBEARD, TERROR OF THE SEAS
by Jean Day

Other Books By The Author:
Sea, Sand, and Settlers
Cedar Island Fisher Folk
Wild Ponies of the Outer Banks
Banker Ponies
Carolina Indians

© 1997 by Jean Day
Library of Congress Catalog Card Number 96-95347
ISBN—1-890238-44-9

Published by Golden Age Press
Stella Day, Publisher
Newport, NC 28570
United States of America
1st Printing----March, 1997
2nd Printing---June, 1997
3rd Printing---April, 2000

Printed by
Griffin & Tilghman Printers, Inc.
New Bern, North Carolina

Publisher
Golden Age Press
599 Roberts Road #11
Newport, North Carolina 28570

TABLE OF CONTENTS

"The love of money is the root of
all evil . . ." I Timothy, 6:10.

INTRODUCTION

Some people through inheritance, luck, or labor
have legally accumulated more wealth than others.
From the beginning of time, this has caused the
"have-nots" to steal from the "haves." When this
happens on land, it's called robbery. When it
occurs on the sea, it's called piracy.

In times of war, when countries were unable
to afford a navy to defend themselves, they
issued, "Letters of Marque," allowing legal
piracy. A percentage of the spoils was to be
awarded to the mother country.

After the war was over, many of the crews of
these ships resorted to piracy, attacking shipping
from all countries, even their own.

The signing of the Peace of Utrecht in 1713
launched the "Golden Age of Piracy." When the
privateers of Queen Anne's War were turned loose,
since they had no place to go and had tasted
the thrill of piracy, they began preying upon
shipping.

The Golden Age of Piracy lasted only five years.

The man who later called himself "Blackbeard"
was one of those privateers. This book, based
on fact and legend, follows the story as it seems
most logical, adding dialogue where it appears
appropriate.

THE MAKING OF A PIRATE

The ragged black flag with the white skull in the center announced their intent. "Fire!" Cannon balls tore through the sails and rigging of the French sloop. The pirate ship pulled alongside. A tall, beefy man heaved grappling hooks across the gap between the two ships. Even as the pirates "Heave--ho-o-ed," drawing the ships closer together, he leaped on board the French sloop, shouting obscenities, firing his pistol. Men screamed in agony as he slashed and chopped human flesh, his cutlass dripping with blood.

As soon as the ships were lashed together, other pirates swarmed over the side. From the pirate sloop Captain Hornigold watched as his men fought, slipping and sliding on the bloody deck, until the captain of the sloop surrendered. It didn't take long.

When it was over, Hornigold met the young man as he jumped back on the pirate ship. "Well done, Teach. This sloop you took--it doesn't seem to be much damaged. It's yours."

The man called Teach carefully hid his elation. "Aye, aye, Sir." He had hoped for a command of his own, but had not expected it to happen so soon.

Edward Drummond watched ships leaving for far ports of the world, dreaming of the day when he could go to sea.

Dozens of stories have been written and told about this man, many true and some no doubt, fictional. But it has been pretty well established that Blackbeard was born Edward Drummond about 1680 in Bristol, England. His parents were respectable, well-to-do, and traveled in high society. His brother was an officer in the artillery. His father told Edward, "When you're old enough, you'll be an army officer like your brother."

"No, Sir, I'll be what I want to be." He was intelligent and personable enough to have become an Army officer, doctor, lawyer, planter, almost anything he decided to become.

"And what do you want to be?"

"I'm going to be a pirate."

His father smiled, "You have plenty of time to change your mind." But Edward, instead of conjugating Latin verbs, preferred to go down to the waterfront and watch ships come from far parts of the world. He would listen spell bound as bronzed, be-whiskered seamen told tales about storms and blood shed and precious jewels and dark-skinned girls.

Bristol was England's second largest city, located where the Avon River meets the Frome River, about eight miles from the Bristol Channel. Since Bristol had the reputation of flooding the seas with privateers and pirates in the seventeenth and early eighteenth centuries, it was not surprising that young Edward chose to follow the sea.

Usually prospective seamen shipped out as cabin boys at the age of twelve, but probably at his father's insistence, young Edward learned all he could before he enlisted. "No matter what

you want to be, education will help." Besides
his regular school work, he devoured every book
or pamphlet he could find about exploration and
buccaneering.

At a time when most men could neither read nor
write, Edward Drummond was an oddity. Portions
of his journals have been found, and he is known
to have corresponded with merchants. In addition,
after his death, a letter addressed to him written
by Tobias Knight, North Carolina's corrupt
Collector of Customs, was found among his
possessions.
In his late teens, Edward became a merchant
seaman. Most of his comrades were rough and
illiterate, groomed in poverty and crime. Although
they came from diverse backgrounds, Edward felt
at home among them, all the while soaking up
knowledge as a rag soaks up spilled rum. He learned
every job on the ship, watched the seas, the
weather, and when possible, he studied the stars
and the charts.
Some time during the later part of Queen Anne's
War (1701-1713), he joined a privateer sailing
out of Kingston, Jamacia to prey upon French
shipping. Since Jamacia is often mentioned in
stories of his life, it is believed his parents
were involved in business there, possibly shipping.
It was acceptable for sons of respectable
families to go to sea, beginning as sailors, then
climbing into positions of authority. Privateering
was considered a contemptible necessity, but
pirating was socially unacceptable.
Edward had a young man's love of adventure and
had found what he wanted to do with his life.
As a privateer, he joined others climbing ropes

to board enemy ships, cutlasses flashing, blood flowing. Edward laughed as men "puked" over the rails at the nauseating odor of blood and death. He learned to differentiate between the various types of ships and which ones were likely to carry valuable cargo.

One source claims that Edward Drummond was, for a time, imprisoned by the French, which left him half-crazed with hatred of that country. This could be true because when he became a pirate, he preyed relentlessly upon French shipping.

At the close of the war, young Drummond suffered from the restlessness common to many young men after being involved in war; he couldn't adjust to peace on land. He began haunting New Providence, a dung heap of former privateers—now pirates—called the "Brethern of the Coast."

The Brethern were American, English, Spanish, French, Dutch, Portuguese, Indian, and African. Over 2,000 pirates lived on board brigatines and sloops in the harbor and in shanties on land. The skeletal remains of over 40 captured ships lay rotting on the beach.

Many of the most notorious pirates made New Providence their home base. They exchanged stories, ate well, drank liberally, and were entertained by young ladies. There were almost as many bars as there were pirates, and the ladies were plentiful, all ages, shapes and colors. Those of mixed races were most in demand.

New Providence was a training school for pirate leaders. Captain Hornigold, the dean of the group, was free with his advice to these novices.

In late 1716, Edward Drummond appeared before Captain Hornigold.

"Speak up, young man."

8

Edward stuttered, in awe of the great man. "I-I want to be a pirate."

Hornigold hid his amusement. This strong, well-bred young man wanted to sign on as a pirate?

"And what is your experience?"

"Merchant seaman and privateer."

"And what is your name?"

"Edward..." Drummond hesitated.

Hornigold watched the young seaman's mind churning, trying to select a new name. He realized his parents would be ashamed when they heard he had finally become a pirate, but he didn't want to embarrass them by using their name. With a new name, his mother and brother wouldn't know about his disgrace, at least for awhile. "Edward Teach."

Most pirates changed their names. If they came from a respectable family, such as Edward Drummond did, it was done to protect their family from embarrassment. They chose names like movie stars did over two hundred years later, names that portrayed who they thought they were, or who they wanted to be. If they survived long enough to stockpile sufficient wealth to retire, using a different name enabled them to return home safely after their pirating days were over.

It is interesting that Drummond adopted the name of Teach since he was such a student. In whatever situation he found himself, he learned from it. Perhaps he secretly aspired to do for others what Hornigold was doing for him, teaching them the finer points of pirating.

In various places, Teach was written Thatch, Tache, Tatch, Tach, or Tash.

Drummond began calling himself Teach and became well known in town, but he remained focused on his goal.

He had been a privateer, but now he would be a pirate.

One of the younger men he met at a bar, asked Teach, "What's the difference between a privateer and a pirate?"

"Well," Teach answered, "I figure it's the same as that of a man and woman who are married living together and two people living together who aren't married. The only difference is a piece of paper."

"There's a little more to it than that," Hornigold said. "A privateer can capture and plunder enemy ships, but he has to turn a certain percentage of the spoils over to the government. Pirates prey upon all shipping, sometimes even from their own country. And they keep all the loot."

Although the pirates Teach associated with were not of the same social class as he was, most of them were honest seamen before becoming pirates. When there were no berths open on merchant ships or jobs available on land, they felt pirating was the only solution to their lives.

At that time, Captain Hornigold was the fiercest, most accomplished pirate of the West Indies. Teach couldn't have chosen a better mentor.

When they sailed out of New Providence in the Bahamas, at last Teach was where he wanted to be. Hornigold was impressed by the young man's intelligence, strength, and bravery. Teach could drink all night and not pass out. He could wield his cutlass with uncanny skill. At in-fighting he was super human. Blood pounded in his temples, his arms and cutlass were one. He was invincible. His comrades, seeing his bravery, willingly followed him into battle.

After Teach was awarded his own sloop, the two captains continued on together. Teach acquired a reputation of his own, rivaling that of Hornigold's, but no jealousy existed between them. New Providence became Teach's home port but he didn't remain there long at any one time. He was well known at the town taverns, but knew what he wanted and was not to be swayed from it. He built a watchtower on a hill outside of town, where he had a panoramic view of the waters of the Bahamas. At the bottom of the hill, where his men erected tents, Teach conducted business, settled disputes, traded goods, made plans, and selected men for the next cruise.

In the spring of 1717, Hornigold told Teach, "It's time to go to sea again. Gather up your men. We'll weigh anchor at dawn."

The two sloops, headed towards the mainland of America. Once on the high seas, they soon captured three small vessels, taking from them one hundred twenty barrels of flour, gallons of wine, and other valuable plunder.

The young boy from Bristol was now a full-fledged pirate.

As Teach's reputation grew, Captain Hornigold bragged, "I taught that boy, Teach, all he knows."

TEACH BECOMES BLACKBEARD

Hornigold and Teach took several rich prizes
and were on their way to New Providence to dispose
of their goods, but their vessels were sluggish.
They sailed into the shallow waters of a cove
until they ran aground. The men made a holiday
of it. A temporary shelter and an earthen fort
were rapidly constructed, fortified by two cannon.
The other cannon, cargo, and heavy gear were moved
to one side, tipping the ship to expose the hull
below the water line. The barnacles and other
marine life were scraped away, then it was daubed
with tallow and sulfur.

When the first side was completed, the process
was repeated on the other side. The crew ate huge
feasts and drank and sang and worked hard until
the job was finished.

Three days later, they were back at sea again,
the ships slipping smoothly through the water.
The lookout on Teach's sloop shouted, "Ship ahead!"

As they drew closer, they could see a large
merchantman flying the French flag. "All hands
to their battle stations!"

The pirates ran up their black flags and rapidly
pursued the ship. Hornigold and Teach worked in
unison.

"He's trying to maneuver into battle position,"
Teach said. "Stand by with your matches ready
to fire!"

Hornigold was now in position. Hornigold and Teach attacked from opposite sides. Shots fired across the bulwarks killed half the sailors and marines. The remainder quickly surrendered.

It was the "Concord," a French guieaman, carrying a cargo of gold dust, money, jewels, and other rich goods from the African coast to the island of Martinique.

After removing the cargo, Hornigold and Teach had to decide what to do with the ship. Should they turn it loose, burn it, or what? Teach suggested, "It's got good lines, probably Dutch built. I want it."

Hornigold studied the young man before him. "There are good reasons we prefer smaller ships. They're easier to maneuver. You saw what happened here. He couldn't move fast enough to get into position to protect himself. A ship this size would have problems in the shallow inlets and channels along the coast. And it, like all ships, will have to be careened. It's size would make this more difficult."

"It would be worth the extra trouble. On the open seas, with the right rigging and me as its master, we would be the terror of the seas," Teach predicted.

So against his better judgment, Hornigold turned the French ship over to Teach.

To make it into a pirate ship, it had to be remodeled. The cabin roof was lowered to make the silhouette less visible from the open seas. This also prevented damage from wooden splinters during battle. The sides and railings were raised, both for protection and for concealment. The sails were rigged to Blackbeard's specifications, and the ship was fitted with 40 guns.

Teach named his new ship the "Queen Anne's Revenge." Pirate ships carried a variety of names but "Revenge" was a favorite, perhaps a statement of their anger against the world which had rejected them.

When they neared New Providence, they met a small pirate sloop. As was the custom, the captain came aboard the "Queen Anne's Revenge" to exchange news. "The King has promised clemency to all pirates who promise to forgo their pirating before September 5th," the captain said.

"So?" Teach raised his thick left eyebrow in derision.

But after their guest had returned to his own sloop, Hornigold told Teach, "It's what I've been waiting for. I've hoarded my loot. I'm going to retire."

And he did. Teach's emotions were mixed. In one way he felt as if he were being deserted by his own father. He realized being completely on his own would present several new problems.

So far most of the important decisions about who to pursue, how to attack, and where to dispose of the loot had been made by Hornigold. And attacking enemy ships using only one vessel meant he had no back up. Yet he was anxious to prove to himself and the world that he was capable of succeeding on his own.

Hornigold and Teach amiably divided their cargo, silver, gold and jewels, and Hornigold sailed into town. Teach sailed out of Nassau on his own to begin his mastery of the seas.

The new governor, Woodes Rogers, came ashore the morning of July 27, 1718. He was in his late thirties and had an outstanding record as a sea captain. His new appointment carried no salary.

Governor Woodes Rogers stood before the old fort
and read his commission to his new subjects.

He received permission to found a plantation colony of 215 European farmers and the materials to establish them. Although he was to share in any profits, his primary concern was to wipe out the pirates from the islands.

Three hundred dirty, drunken pirates formed two scraggly lines from the waterfront to the fort. The fort was in poor repair, not fit for occupancy. It would be interesting to know what Rogers and the other dignitaries thought when they saw the large gathering of pirates. But they marched safely between the honor guard while being saluted with musket shots fired over their heads.
Rogers with great dignity, unrolled a scroll and in a loud solemn voice read his commission from it.
As soon as the service was over, Rogers met with Hornigold. "Where is your cohort--Teach? I didn't see him among the pirates."
"He refused to accompany me here to greet you. And there are several others absent also, notably Charles Vane." Hornigold wanted to draw the governor's attention away from Teach.
An aide handed Rogers a sealed message. He broke it open. "It seems a group of pirates led by Charles Vane are anchored in the bay and wish to discuss terms for their surrender."
"Is there an answer?" the aide asked.
"No answer. The only terms I will accept from Charles Vane or any other pirate is complete capitulation." He turned to Hornigold, "I come prepared to deal with miscreants like him."
The new governor was backed up by a convoy of British warships--the frigates "Milford" and "Rose" and the sloops "Buck" and "Shark."

As the sloops came into the harbor, Rogers watched helplessly. "He's moving the prize ship directly across from my fleet. What do you suppose he thinks he's doing?"

"The guns on the ship are aimed at your sloops," Hornigold said. "He's going to attack.

Rogers watched through his spyglass. "They're leaving in small boats. I wonder why?"

Seconds later the answer came. The silence of the black tropical night was rent with deafening explosions. Flames leaped high into the sky, lighting up the whole harbor. "That sea scum Vane must have loaded her with explosives, then set her afire!" Hornigold was shocked but had to admire his former comrade's audacity.

"He's cut her loose. She's drifting towards the 'Rose.'" It was the truth. The captains of both the "Rose" and the "Shark" had been forced to flee to avoid the burning fire ship. The blazing inferno effectively blocked the harbor, allowing Vane and his friends to escape. Charles Vane ran up his black flag, fired a salute of derision at the British fleet, raised sail and made his way out to the open sea.

Rogers ordered his aide, "Send the 'Rose' and the 'Shark' after him." But it was to no avail. Later he sent Hornigold out with the same mission, but he too failed to capture the errant pirate.

The crowds of former pirates were milling about the island, drinking and fighting and whoring. To keep them busy and give them encouragement, he offered them a small plot of land if they would clear the land and build a house upon it within one year.

After many years of adventure, Hornigold found life on land dull, so he began aiding Governor

Woodes Rogers capture the remaining pirates. Rogers was wise enough to realize it took a master pirate to catch pirates and sent him out after Charles Vane and other notorious pirates. Hornigold was one of the few pardoned pirates who did not recant his vows.

While serving as a seaman, privateer, and carousing in the taverns of New Providence, Teach had studied what made a pirate captain successful. He saw what worked for others and where they made mistakes. Pirate ships were like small democracies where the leaders and other important matters were usually voted upon. If the men were dissatisfied with their share of the loot or conditions aboard the ship, they elected a new captain. If the old captain agreed with their decision, there was no problem. But if he objected, he was disposed of—shot, stabbed, thrown overboard to feed the sharks or left marooned on a small island to starve.

Teach intended to remain as captain. It was not a position he had been elected to; Hornigold had appointed him. Since pirates were such a blood thirsty, cruel lot, he deliberately created an image so horrifying that his men would hold him in such awe, they would obey his every command without an argument. He was almost seven feet tall. His enormous stature and strength made a good beginning.

The next vessel they encountered was a British merchant vessel. The crew was quickly subdued. "Bring the captain aboard the 'Queen Anne's Revenge,'" Teach ordered.

He was a short, well endowed man, dressed in his dress blue uniform, his hat set at precisely the correct angle, his boots highly polished.

When Teach stood up to greet him, the poor man trembled with fright. His sword clattered to the deck. "Surely this isn't a man at all, it's Satan," he muttered to himself.

Teach was enough to frighten the bravest of men. While at this time, most men didn't wear beards, Teach's beard was grizzly and black. His hair had grown long. It was braided into little pigtails, some of which were tied with brightly colored ribbons, while others were swept back behind his ears. His thick, bushy eye brows emphasized his piercing, cruel eyes and evil grin. Under his hat, on each side of his face, dangled cords of hemp dipped in a solution of saltpeter and lime water. They smoldered like a fuse, wreathing his head in sulfurous smoke. He carried heavy artillery, including an enormous jeweled cutlass. He looked like the Devil Incarnate.

"I am known as Blackbeard, King of the Seas. And who are you?" This was the first time Teach had called himself Blackbeard, but he felt comfortable with his new name.

The other captain was too frightened to speak. Liquid streamed down his pants leg, leaving a yellow puddle behind on the deck as he turned and ran, escaping towards his own vessel. Blackbeard allowed him to go, guffawing at his fright.

As time went on, Blackbeard refined his appearance. The main source of information on Blackbeard is a book written in 1724 by Captain Samuel Johnson (he was believed to have been Daniel DeFoe).

He says, "...from that large quantity of hair which, like a frightful meteor, covered his whole face and frightened America more than any comet

that has appeared there [in] a long time."
Atop his wild midnight black hair, Blackbeard
wore a broad black hat. His bright colored silk
or velvet jacket was full skirted with chunky
cuffs reaching way up to his elbows. At times,
he covered this with a scarlet cloak. His knee
britches were of clashing bright colors, and he
wore huge silver buckles on his low-cut shoes.
Although his appearance was startling, it was
his charisma which made him who he was. When
he entered a room, all eyes were upon him and
conversation stopped. He was liked by those who
knew him almost as much as he was feared. His
reputation had become his most important asset.
It kept his men in line and made his enemies cower.
With the capture of each ship, Blackbeard's
reputation grew.

Blackbeard manned his ship with 300 men, some
from the former crew of the "Concord," his own
crew, and cutthroats and thieves gathered from
the other islands.

Near the island of St. Vincent, dead ahead,
they sighted a large, tall, heavily armed merchant
ship, the "Great Allen." After fierce fighting,
Captain Taylor surrendered.

Blackbeard ordered him, "Move your ship closer
to shore, then tell your men to get off."

Taylor obeyed. "And what of my vessel?"

"I'll do with it as I please. Any objections?"

Of course there were none. While the cargo was
transferred from the "Great Allen" to the "Queen
Anne's Revenge," Blackbeard entertained Captain
Taylor in his cabin. Taylor showed no fear when
he encountered his host, but he sat at the edge
of his seat. After a brief interview, Blackbeard
dismissed Taylor and sent him ashore with his

crew to either starve or be rescued by a passing ship.

Blackbeard allowed his men to choose rewards from the loot. Among the items he claimed for himself, was a fine silver cup. He brought out barrels of rum. The pirates' wild celebration could be heard from the shore. Flames from the burning "Great Allen" roared and crackled, rising high into the midnight sky, visible for miles around.

News of his victory over the "Great Allen" soon spread, adding greatly to the reputation of Blackbeard.

Soon after this, Blackbeard's lookout shouted, "Ho! Man-of-war approaching." It was the 30 gun British "Scarborough," hunting the "Queen Anne's Revenge" with specific orders to hunt and destroy.

Navigator Israel Hands said, "We're out-gunned. She must have 30 cannon."

Others said, "Let's turn tail and show them our wake."

Blackbeard knew he could have out-sailed the other ship, but he didn't. "No man can say Blackbeard ran from a fight." Instead, he held his fire as the "Scarborough" fired their long range guns at him.

"Shouldn't we answer fire?" Hands asked.

"Not yet."

When the "Scarborough" was close enough, Blackbeard ordered, "Fire broadside!" Large holes were ripped in the sails of the warship. The explosion was so loud, he felt his ears pop. As Blackbeard closed in, the warship fired again, striking the mast and shredding the top sails of the "Queen Anne's Revenge."

The battle continued for several hours until

Blackbeard had begun to wonder if the he was capable of defeating the British warship. Then suddenly the "Scarborough" turned tail to return to Barbados Island to report the failure of their expedition.

Blackbeard shouted in glee, "Run you scurvy scum. No one can defeat me, Blackbeard, Terror of the Seas."

Excited by the battle, some of the pirates wanted to pursue the man-of-war. But not Blackbeard. "I don't run, but neither do I risk the "Queen Anne's Revenge" for a ship that contains no cargo."

He saluted the defeated warship with one final salvo and turned towards the Spanish settlements of South America. Word of his defeat of the British warship spread throughout the Atlantic.

Blackbeard was truly an invincible commander. His awesome appearance and ferocious actions caused the crews of many ships to refuse to fight him. The men were poorly paid and not anxious to lose their lives fighting a losing battle against such a beast. Sailors were superstitious, and this man put the fear of the devil in them.

There are many stories about the cruelty of Blackbeard. He was cruel. But in the beginning he did this with an evil desire to impress others of his cruelty.

After boarding a passenger vessel, he went about taking money and jewelry from his victims. He halted before a muscular belligerent man. "Give me your ring." It was a huge ruby on the man's left pinkie finger.

"No way. If you want my ring, you'll have to take it off."

"Have it your way." Blackbeard grabbed the man's hand and placed it on a barrel. He withdrew his huge knife with the jeweled handle from his belt, and with one swift movement he chopped off the offending finger. He put the ring on his own pinkie finger. It stuck past the first joint, so he left it there, then tossed the unlucky man's finger over the rail. After that, no one argued, but voluntarily produced their valuables.

The writer Johnson tells the story of what happened one day when they were becalmed and the men were restless. Blackbeard opened a keg of rum. After they had become a little flushed with drink, he said, "Come let's make a hell of our own, and try how long we can bear it."

So he and two or three others went down into the hold. He closed up all the hatches, then filled several pots to the top with brimstone and other combustible matter. To the consternation of his companions, he set the pots on fire. Black smoke erupted from the smoldering pots and filled the small enclosure. The other men cried out, "Air! We need air!"

But Blackbeard calmly ignored their discomfort, an evil grin on his face. Then when the men were coughing, choking for air, almost suffocated, he opened the hatches to allow fresh air to come in.

"I, Blackbeard, am the strongest, bravest of them all!"

One day Blackbeard, Israel Hands, and two other men were in Blackbeard's cabin, sitting at his table, drinking. Suddenly Blackbeard pulled out a pair of pistols and cocked them under the table.

One man, fearful of what he suspected was going to happen, leapt to his feet and backed out of the cabin. Blackbeard blew out the candle, crossed his arms under the table, and pulled the triggers

of both guns at the same time. One misfired, but
the slug from the other one tore into Hands' knee,
crippling him for life.

When asked why he would do such a heinous thing,
he answered, "If I didn't kill one of them from
time to time, they would forget who I am."

The young boy from Bristol had become the most
fearsome pirate of them all.

Several times each year, it became necessary for the pirates to careen their vessels. They sailed close to shore, then moved the heavy cargo and guns to the side of the ship nearest shore, tipping the vessel, thus allowing the men to scrape off the barnacles and other sea life from the bottom of the ship.

PARDON AT BATH

During his short career (15 to 18 months as a pirate captain), Blackbeard successfully captured and plundered more than his share of ships. In December of 1717, he stopped the merchant ship, "Margaret," and removed her cargo of cattle and hogs. As Captain Bostock watched, two of his crew members appeared before Blackbeard.

The King of the Pirates stared at them. He knew their minds, but he wanted them to ask. "Speak up, men. What's the problem?"

The taller of the two, turning his face away from his captain, spoke for them both. "We want to join up with you."

"What's the matter? Is Bostock too rough on you?" Blackbeard roared with laughter. "Hey, Israel, put these two miserable hands to work swabbing the deck. And see to it that they do a proper job of it."

Then he allowed Captain Bostock to leave with his ship and crew unharmed and grateful to be alive, even though they were left unarmed.

When Captain Bostock reached land, he reported the incident to the authorities. "I was invited into the captain's cabin. The vessel was either French or Dutch. I saw one sloop alongside. The captain told me that he had over 300 men with him." The number of crew members fluctuated according to who was doing the estimating, and

whom he was trying to impress. Then too, the
number changed as some men were killed or left
behind and others joined up.

"He showed me some silver he had, including
a fine silver cup he said he took from Captain
Taylor. I told him about the offer of pardon
being sent out from London for all pirates who
would take the oath. But he didn't act like he
was interested," he said.

During December of 1717 and January of 1718,
Blackbeard continued to cruise in the same area
because the hunting was good.

As time progressed, Blackbeard was becoming
more and more the villain he displayed to the
world. The softer side of his nature almost
disappeared except when it concerned the "wenches."
The constant killing and the bickering among his
men was beginning to bother him. In a fragment
of his journal, he says:

"Such a Day...Rum all out...Our company
somewhat sober: Rogues plotting...great talk of
Separation...So I look'd Sharp for a prize."

Having experienced it himself, Blackbeard knew
what a sailor's life was all about. Long hours
of hard labor, hours of dull monotony, poor food,
no privacy, hard taskmasters, all for little pay.

To maintain control of his men and to keep them
primed up, he kept them well supplied with liquor.
After he had successfully captured a merchant
ship and replenished the supply of liquor, he
wrote:

"Such a Day, took one with a great deal of Liquor
on board, so kept the company hot, Damn'd Hot.
Then all things went well again."

In January, Blackbeard sailed into Bath Town,
North Carolina. He had been there before. This

was where Governor Eden made his home and conducted business. At that time the government had no permanent home.

According to Jack Goodwin, of Sea Level, Captain Josiah Jones, one of his ancestors, was one of the first settlers of Bath Town. Jones was a wealthy shipper and plantation owner until he lost much of his wealth because of pirates.

One of the early residents was Christopher Gale, the colony's first Chief Justice, who owned the Kirby-Grange house in 1708.

In 1701, John Lawson, explorer, mapmaker, botanist, ethnologist, and author built a house on Back Creek for himself and his female companion, Hannah Smith. In 1705-06 Bath Town became the oldest incorporated town and port in North Carolina. It was hoped that since all shipping from both the Neuse and Pamlico Rivers had to go to Bath, the town would prosper and grow. In 1707 a grist mill and ship yard were established. The strength of the town was weakened by political rivalry, epidemics, and Indian Wars.

In 1711, when the Tuscarora Indians attacked, those from the surrounding area sought shelter in the town. John Lawson had been traveling among the Indians and wasn't worried since he considered them his friends. That is, until, at the beginning of the Indian Wars, when he was captured and roasted alive.

When Blackbeard came to Bath Town, he pushed his way past the governor's aide into Governor Eden's office. Governor Eden could scarcely believe what he saw. This man towering above him had to be Blackbeard, King of the Pirates. He had some nerve appearing here in his executive office. Eden almost arrested him then and there,

A Spanish Galleon

but he decided to wait and see what this blackguard had to say.

After preliminary greetings, Blackbeard seated himself without an invitation. "I've come for my pardon."

Blackbeard, Terror of the Seas, was asking for a pardon? Eden was tempted to immediately place him in irons, but the royal edict was explicit. Any pirate who asked for pardon was to receive it. He had no choice but to comply. "Do you swear to give up pirating and will you sign an oath to that effect?"

"If I do, am I free to leave with the 'Queen Anne's Revenge?'"

"This calls for further discussion." They wrangled over who was to receive how much but eventually came to an equitable agreement. Neither Eden nor Blackbeard believed the oath would be kept.

Blackbeard had no intention of giving up pirating, so it is curious that he even asked for it. But if the goods he carried were declared legal, then he could sell them without having to return to Cuba or the other islands.

He lingered around Bath Town, where he openly peddled his merchandise for reduced prices. Plantation owners and businessmen willingly paid higher prices for the pirate loot than the professional fences would have in the Bahamas. Since England charged such a high tariff on their goods, the settlers were pleased to avoid paying the exorbitant prices she demanded.

Many settlers accepted the pirates, secretly admiring them.

Off the mainland of North Carolina are its fabled Outer Banks, wide beaches of sand dunes, scattered grasses and salt marsh. It offered a safe haven for pirates, easy shelter in its many coves and inlets. Traffic between the Atlantic Ocean and Pamlico Sound had to pass through Old Ocracoke Inlet. Because of shifting inlets and channels, even experienced seamen required local men to pilot them through. So either Blackbeard had men with him who knew the inlets or else he picked up one or more to use as pilots while he was there.

People from Cedar Island say that when Blackbeard needed help, he would stop off at Cedar Island to pick up one of the Day men, probably to be used as pilots.

Blackbeard remained in the area until March of 1718. He became acquainted with the residents at this time. Records are almost non-existent, but they show that the area was thinly populated by a variety of poverty stricken individuals.

Where did these hardy souls come from? Shipwrecks were common. This was called the "Graveyard of the Atlantic." Survivors swam or were washed ashore, where they remained. Many of those presently living there claim their ancestors were pirates Blackbeard left stranded on the Outer Banks. They were joined by runaways, criminals, and slaves. They used what they could salvage from ship wrecks to build and furnish their homes. They raised gardens and hunted and fished, eking out an existence. Life was tough.

In 1728, William Byrd described two of those who lived on Currituck:

"On the South Shore, not far from the Inlet, dwelt a Marooner, that Modestly call'd himself a Hermit, tho' he forfeited that Name by Suffering a wanton female to cohabit with Him. His habitation was a Bower, cover'd with bark after

Indian fashion, which in that mild Situation protected him pretty well from the weather. Like Ravens, he neither plow'd nor sow'd, but subsisted chiefly upon Oysters, which his Handmaid made Shift to gather from the Adjacent rocks. Sometimes for the change of Dyet, he sent her to drive up the Neighbor's cows to moisten their Mouths with a little Milk. But as for rainment, he depended mostly upon his Length of Beard, and She upon her Length of hair, part of which she brought decently forward, and the rest dangled behind quite down to her Rump."

Or, as Robert Day puts it:

"There once was a man on Currituck,
Who lived on the oysters his woman'd shuck.
    No clothes did they wear
    Except for their hair,
And hers blew in the wind when he had
                                    any luck."

One occupation practiced by these hardy men and women was on an even keel with pirating. It was called wrecking. Near Currituck is a place called Nag's head. David Stick, in his <u>Outer Banks of North Carolina</u>, has an interesting story as to where it got its name.

According to him, the name came from a trick used to lure vessels to destruction. A Banks pony was driven up and down the beach at night, with a lantern tied about its neck. The up and down motion of the pony resembled that of a vessel, causing unsuspecting seamen to steer towards it, thinking it was a safe channel. It would run aground, often breaking up on the dangerous shoals. Then the robbers would set to and steal anything they could salvage, killing any survivors. They had no deck beneath them or black flag flying above them, but they were still pirates.

According to Mrs. Victoria Pruit, Chincoteague island historian, the early families in that area lived in one room huts with a dirt floor, one window and the one door hung with wooden shingles. The fireplace was simply shells or stones piled in a corner. Smoke escaped through a hole in the roof. When the fire didn't provide sufficient light, they burned pieces of sheep's wool in a clam shell filled with bayberries or hog's lard or mutton tallow. These were called "Sows."

So these weren't the sort of people who would report the presence of pirates in the area. They welcomed them and traded fresh meat and sea food for needed supplies. Blackbeard knew some of these people and visited in their homes. He was as welcome there as he was in the finest homes of the planters in Bath Town or Edenton. Older inhabitants of that area say their grandparents told about the foreign goods Blackbeard brought and how welcome they were.

He tarried a few weeks, then about the first of March, he set sail for the Bay of Honduras.

STEDE BONNET, GENTLEMAN PIRATE

Blackbeard soon ignored the pardon so graciously given by Governor Eden.

The Bay of Honduras was a favorite gathering place for the pirates. After leaving Bath Town, Blackbeard headed that way. Several miles out, the lookout spotted a sloop coming towards them. As it drew closer, they could see it carried a black flag and ten guns.

Blackbeard ordered his Jolly Roger raised and invited the captain of the other ship aboard the "Queen Anne's Revenge."

The captain of the sloop used his bull horn to inquire, "And to whom do I have the pleasure of speaking?"

Blackbeard roared with laughter. This funny little potbellied man in a red waistcoat, tan britches, with no beard, wearing what was obviously a wig and with the prissy way of speaking, dared to ask Blackbeard, King of the Seas, who he was?

Blackbeard answered, "A Gentleman of the Brethern. Prepare to come aboard." Even the odd little captain in the other vessel, understood this was an order.

Although they had never met before, Bonnet surely recognized Blackbeard since his reputation went far and wide. He accepted the invitation to come on board and awkwardly climbed from one ship to the other.

When Blackbeard met with the other captain in

34

Captain Stede Bonnet, Gentleman Pirate

his cabin, he was startled to discover the other
man was Major Stede Bonnet, as Doctor Charles
Johnson says, "lately a gentleman of good
reputation and estate." He was from the West
Indian Island of Barbadas.

As they talked, Blackbeard learned more about
this incredible pirate captain. He listened in
amazement as Bonnet told him a little of his story.
He came from a well-respected, well-to-do family.
Perhaps their parents were acquainted. Bonnet
had led a sheltered life, was well-educated.
This drew Blackbeard to him. It reminded him
of his own boyhood. He wasn't about to admit
it to anyone, but he missed that part of his life.

Bonnet had been an Army officer. Blackbeard's
brother was an Army officer. When Bonnet retired
from the Army, he had settled down on a sugar
plantation, where he married Mary Allamby, probably
the woman his parents had chosen for him. Four
children were born, three boys and one girl.
He had become quite wealthy. "But this was not
enough. It was the same thing day after day.
I longed for adventure."

Blackbeard recognized the longings in this
strange man, the same longings he had experienced
himself when he was a youth.

"So where did you get your sloop?"

"I bought it at an auction. It had been found
deserted at sea without a crew or papers."

"And you believed that?"

"Of course. Why not?"

Blackbeard laughed so hard, he strangled, then
sputtered, "You mean you actually bought your
own ship? No one has ever done that before.
We capture them or we steal them. A pirate never
pays for his own ship."

Then smothering his amusement, he asked, "What did your family think of that?"

"No problem. When they questioned me about it, I told them I planned to establish a trade route between islands. Then I hired on a crew..."

"You hired a crew?"

"Of course. I frequented the taverns and grog shops of Bridgeton and hired about seventy men. The man I hired as quartermaster was experienced and knew what to do."

Blackbeard stifled his laughter. This man was a riot. It had been years since he had had so much fun. "How did your crew react when they found out you wanted them to become pirates?"

"They voted on it. Can you imagine that?"

He persuaded Bonnet to join forces with him. "Two pirate ships working in unison is much more effective than operating seperately." Life would never be dull with this buffoon around. They joined forces in their quest for gold.

The two ships sailed out in tandem. Since Bonnet's ship was named the "Revenge," to avoid confusion, Blackbeard sometimes referred to his own as the "Queen Anne." Through the next weeks, Blackbeard learned more about Bonnet. He had become so fed up with his nagging wife and monotonous life that one night he simply had had enough. He weighed anchor and went out to sea Without even a word of farewell to his wife or friends.

"What do you suppose they thought when you left like that?"

"I don't know and I don't care. I've done what others wanted all my life, first my parents, then my wife. It was time I did what I wanted."

He bragged, "And so far, I've been successful

at it."

From Barbados, with his motley crew, he had set out for the coast of Virginia. A few days out at sea, he had the thrill of capturing his first ship, the "Anne" of Glassgow. He had found himself. This was what he wanted. Euphoric, his luck continued.

When he sighted the "Turbes," he recognized it was from Barbados, possibly even owned by an acquaintance. He plundered the ship, keeping the cargo, set the crew ashore, then he burned the ship. From then on, every ship he found from his home port, Barbados, he burned. If he thought this would keep his family and former friends from discovering where he was and what he was doing, he was mistaken. The men he left stranded on an island, had hailed a passing ship and been rescued.

They carried news of Major Stede Bonnet and his pirate ship, the "Revenge." When word arrived in Bridgeport that Stede Bonnet, former Army officer, wealthy plantation owner—that respectable pinnacle of manhood—had become a bloody, despicable pirate, it caused a furor which rippled through the islands. Some suggested that, "Poor Bonnet be tetched in the head from too much sun." Others said it differently, "Humour of going pyrating, proceeded from a Disorder of his Mind."

At the beginning everything had gone well on the "Revenge," until the crew became irritated with their amateur captain. They wanted their share of the loot instead of a measly salary. Bonnet was a bungling idiot. He had never even been to sea before and knew absolutely nothing about navigation or controlling men. As an officer in the British Army, he was in charge of many soldiers, but this was different. These men were different, mostly ignorant, quarrelsome criminals.

The crew of the "Revenge" was on the verge of mutiny when Bonnet joined up with Blackbeard. At first Blackbeard just thought Bonnet was odd, but it took only a few days before he realized what a strange partner he had acquired. He was amusing, but he was incompetent.

So he suggested to Bonnet, "A man of your stature shouldn't have to deal with such unruly men. You deserve a life of ease. Let me take care of that mutinous crew of yours. I know how to handle such rough men. You sit back and enjoy the scenery. Of course you will still collect your captain's share."

Bonnet wasn't stupid, just naive. He understood what Blackbeard was saying, but there was nothing he could do but comply. The lack of money wasn't the reason he became a pirate, and he had brought with him more than he needed. He realized he could not depend on any assistance from his own crew. From that time on, he was a virtual prisoner on board the "Queen Anne."

He watched as Blackbeard took over his sloop and appointed Lieutenant Richards to command it. The crew welcomed a seasoned commander, and the threat of mutiny passed. At least for awhile. Bonnet remained on board the "Queen Anne" as the ships went on their way. He spent his time reading and brooding.

Twelve vessels of various sizes were captured.

While watering at Turniff, the lookout spied another large vessel with four smaller sloops also seeking water. It was the British sloop, "Adventure." Blackbeard hoisted his black flag with a complete skeleton on it and fired at them.

Since escape was impossible, and he wasn't stupid enough to attempt to attack such superior force, the master of the ship, David Harriot, signaled his surrender. Harriot and his men fled ashore, but he was ordered aboard the "Queen Anne." A rope ladder was thrown over the side for him.

Blackbeard liked the way the man had yielded to his superior force, yet now he stood tall with his hand on the hilt of his sword. "I'm going to make you an offer I've never made to a captain of a captured vessel before. Would you like to join forces with me?"

Harriot didn't hesitate. "I think I can speak for my men. We will be honored to serve you."

Israel Hands was placed in command of the "Adventure." It was manned by half the original crew and half taken from the other ships.

Blackbeard had a long memory. Because some pirates had recently been hanged in Boston, Blackbeard burned the ship which was from there and allowed the others to go.

Blackbeard, who was now in charge of four ships, began calling himself, the Commodore. He prowled up and down the coast, overcoming any ships that came his way, regardless of nationality; Spanish, French, British, or American.

Bonnet was living a life of ease, while Richards ably commanded his ship. He was dissatisfied with the situation, but he had learned early in life to accept whatever life dealt him, only revolting when he had gone to sea as a self-styled pirate. But now, he accepted what he couldn't change.

THE SIEGE OF CHARLES TOWNE

Near the last of May, 1718, Blackbeard anchored his ships off the port of Charles Towne, South Carolina. Gazing through his spyglass, he viewed the city spread before him with numerous ships anchored in the harbor. This was the busiest port in the South.

Charles Towne had been settled by the English in 1670. In the early eighteenth century, piracy was more or less encouraged by the merchants despite vigorous objections from London. For a time, pirate ships docked at Charles Towne harbor while pirates strolled unconcernedly down its brick streets. After the colony's legislature passed laws restricting their activities, the pirates were no longer seen in town.

But when Blackbeard arrived, the city of Charles Towne was unprotected. Since it was still recovering from wars with the Indians, it was incapable of defending itself. And there were no British war ships in the harbor. Blackbeard wondered what it would it be like to make this city bow low before him.

As he stood there, contemplating his next action, the ship's surgeon, Doctor Cabot, appeared before him. "The men are murmuring again. There is much sickness among them."

"See to it, Man. Do your job. I can't be bothered with details."

The ship's surgeon had been with Blackbeard
for awhile and dared to speak up. "I would,
Commodore, but we are almost out of medical
supplies. I need medicines if I am to treat them."
    "And where am I to obtain them?" Ah-h, the
city of Charles Towne would have medicines. But
when Blackbeard saw a pilot boat approaching from
the harbor, he put the problem of the sick men
out of his mind.
    The boat was easily overcome, and the pilot
brought on board. If he decided to enter the
harbor, this man would be his passport into the
city. They seized a vessel entering the harbor,
then a brigatine carrying fourteen slaves, then
another vessel rich with gold.
    The lookout spied the ship, "Crowley," commanded
by Captain Robert Clark, leaving on its way to
London. Blackbeard's reputation was such by this
time, that Captain Clark surrendered without a
battle. This ship was a real find. Not only
were its coffers filled with gold and silver and
jewels, it contained some of Charles Towne's
leading citizens, including Samuel Wragg, a member
of the Council of the Province of South Carolina.
He was accompanied by his four year old son
William. Wragg was an important hostage, a bargain
in Blackbeard's game of chess.
    Blackbeard ordered the prisoners brought before
him. "How many ships are there in the harbor?
What is their cargo and destination?"
    No one answered.
    "I want the truth. If you refuse to answer
or if you lie, I promise you that you will be
keel-hauled. If you've never seen a man after
he has been dragged back and forth under the ship
from one side to the other, the result of scraping

against barnacles leaves one bloody mess."

The prisoners all looked to Samuel Wragg to speak for them. He stepped forward and gave Blackbeard the information he desired.

"Throw the passengers into the hold with the cargo," Blackbeard ordered.

"But surely not myself or my young son," Wragg protested.

"Everyone." Men of quality were ordinarily given special privileges when captured.

The hold was damp and dark and cold and crowded. Terror seized the prisoners—they were certain they were going to be killed.

Blackbeard stopped every ship coming in or going out of the harbor. Within a few days, he and his men had captured eight or nine ships. This halted commerce completely. No vessels dared to enter. And none dared to leave.

Doctor Cabot once more appeared before Blackbeard. "The men are complaining of malaria and festered wounds and the usual results from comporting with diseased wenches. We must have medicines or risk a mutiny."

"All you had to do was ask. Make out a list of the tinctures and ointments you need."

"But where will you get them?"

"Stop whining and bring me the list."

Then Blackbeard ordered Samuel Wragg and several other prisoners of importance brought before him. "You are my hostages. I am sending Lieutenant Richards and seaman Jones into the city to obtain the medicines we need. If the governor does not fill my order immediately, then I—like King Herod of old—shall have your heads delivered to the governor on a silver platter—and burn the city."

The men shook with fear. Some almost fainted.

"Who among you is willing to go with my men to convince the governor I mean business?"

Samuel Wragg volunteered. But Blackbeard vetoed this. Wragg was his most important prisoner. The governor might not allow him to return. A man named Marks was chosen. The crew voted to accept him as their representative.

As Marks and the two pirates prepared to go, Blackbeard warned them, "I am giving you two days to see the governor and bring back the medicine. If either of my men fails to return, I will burn every ship in the harbor and leave nothing of the city but ashes."

Then Blackbeard placed his own scarlet cloak around Marks' shoulders to prove to the governor that this man spoke with his authority.

Blackbeard moved his flotilla five or six leagues from land and waited. The hours passed slowly. At the end of two days, there was no sign of the boat's return. He called Wragg before him. Glaring furiously at him, he declared, "Prepare to die!"

"But, Sir, something unforeseen might have occurred. Possibly the medicines were not readily available."

Blackbeard was not anxious to kill his prisoners or to burn the city. What he wanted was for them to fear him. The power he held was like an aphrodisiac to his ego.

The whole ship, passengers and crew alike, collectively held their breaths the next day. As Blackbeard paced the deck, men scurried out of his path.

Towards nightfall, the lookout shouted, "Small boat approaching from the harbor!"

"All men report to your stations!"

As the boat drew closer, the men could see

Blackbeard's cloak on the shoulders of the lone
man in the boat. But the man was not Marks, he
was a common seaman. "Where are Lieutenant Richards
and the medicine chest?" Doctor Cabot asked,
twisting his hat he held in his hands.

Some of the pirates wanted to kill the seaman
without further ado, but Blackbeard protested,
"Hold. Let this man have his say."
The man was so frightened he could barely speak,
but he managed to tell his story.
"I were out in my boat fishing as I always does,
when I seen a man on a hatch with two seamen
pushing it through the water. It were Mr. Marks.
His boat had turned over in a squall. The men
was trying to push him toward the city. They paid
me to come tell you. Another fisher boat took
them on into the city."
Blackbeard was tired of waiting. Was the governor
dallying with him? Israel Hands suggested, "I'd
hang him up from the yardarm if 'twas me."
"But you're not me, are you?" Blackbeard wasn't
going to be told what he should do. "Fetch me
some ale. Get this creature some food. Then give
the prisoners the run of the ship. I'll allow
them two more days."
This wasn't a popular idea with the crew, but
like Blackbeard said, he was the captain.
Blackbeard spent the next two days drinking with
Israel Hands and a huge man called Black Ceasar.
At the end of that time, he swore he would kill
the hostages and any other South Carolinian he
could lay his hands on.
But Samuel Wragg pleaded, "Please give them
one more night. They might return tonight."
Satisfied that he had brought this important

man begging at his feet, he agreed.

The prisoners were certain death was near. They held a meeting, then sent a spokesman to speak to Blackbeard. "The governor done us wrong. If you'll give us our lives, we'll serve you with ours. We'll pilot your ships into the harbor and lead you in the attack of the town."

Sniveling idiots! Why couldn't they stand up like men and take what they deserved?

But in the city, they were not deliberately dawdling over the issue. Some of the medicines were not available and they were having difficulty finding suitable substitutes. Governor Johnson and his Council did not want to give into Blackbeard's demands, but they had no choice. There was no way they could prevent Blackbeard from entering the town and sacking it at will.

Meanwhile Richards and Jones swaggered down the brick street and in and out of the taverns of the town.

Blackbeard had lost his patience. "Enough time wasted over this thing. It's time for action."

During the night they moved closer to town. When the sun rose over Charles Towne Harbor, those watching anxiously from the shore, saw four pirate ships and four captive ships lined up in the harbor, facing the city, their cannon aimed towards the waterfront.

"Let them try to hide, but there'll be no hiding places." The power Blackbeard felt was making him feel giddy.

Governor Johnson sent word that he was collecting the medicines, and Mr. Marks was preparing to leave immediately. But Lieutenant Richards and seaman Jones were nowhere to be found. Marks wouldn't dare return without them. If he did, he would surely be killed. Blackbeard would think the governor had thrown them in jail or killed them. Finally the missing men were found in a tavern, boisterous and drunk, spinning tales of killing and robbery to their mesmerized drinking companions. Richards and Jones were carried out to the long boat to be returned to the pirate ships.

After Marks arrived with the medicine, including mercury to treat syphilis, Blackbeard released his prisoners, allowing them to take their ship after it had been stripped of all valuables. Since the crew had taken most of their clothing, the hostages were half naked when they left.

The medical supplies Marks brought were not all that expensive. They could have been purchased elsewhere. But once Blackbeard had made up his mind about something, he was not to be deterred from his decisions.

Governor Johnson now knew that HE, BLACKBEARD, was not a man to be trifled with. "Prepare to come about," Blackbeard ordered.

The time spent at Charles Towne Harbor had not been wasted. While there, he had captured eight or nine ships, one of their richest hauls yet. Their coffers were over-flowing and the hold was crammed full with sundry merchandise.

The people of Charles Towne were angry and mortified. They were determined that never again would they be held hostage by a pirate.

Pleased with his success at Charles Towne, Blackbeard headed back up the coast to Old Topsail Inlet, his already fierce reputation greatly augmented.

BEAUFORT, "HONGRY TOWNE" BY THE SEA

Beaufort, the third oldest town in North Carolina, nestles inside Old Topsail Inlet. For a time it was called Port Beaufort, but in Blackbeard's time it wasn't yet an official port. In fact, it wasn't much of anything.

Beaufort was surveyed and laid out by Richard Graves in October of 1713. The words "Hongry Towne" and Hungry Towne" were scratched on the side of the official survey document. Although this was apparently only doodling, it does give us a hint of what Beaufort was like at that time.

When Blackbeard visited there in 1718, Beaufort was still struggling to exist.

From earliest Colonial days, Old topsail Inlet, now known as Beaufort Inlet, offered a relatively safe haven from coastal Carolina storms. Pirates used Core Sound and Cape Lookout Bight to careen their ships and restock them with water and meat. Cape Lookout Bight was the nursing ground for the whales as they migrated north.

On a hammock east of what was the official town limits, stood a large white two story wooden house called the Hammock House. No one knows exactly when it was built or by whom. One theory is that the house was constructed by ship captains or pirates to be used as an inn (ordinary). It remains standing, the oldest house in Beaufort.

Because of its location and height, it was visible from a considerable distance and served

48

Tradition says that while in Beaufort, Blackbeard stayed at Hammock House, the oldest house in Beaufort.

as a shipping landmark for those wanting to enter Old Topsail Inlet.

In Blackbeard's time the land upon which it was built was owned by Robert Turner. It is doubtful if Blackbeard or any other pirate would construct such a fine house as this one was on property not owned by them.

It can not be compared with the mansions along the James River in Virginia or at Edenton in North Carolina, but nevertheless it was and is both impressive and utilitarian.

The house was apparently built by ship's carpenters. It has a double front porch which is typical of Bahamian style architecture. The timbers are mostly Scottish heart pine, joined together by hand hewn pegs. Recently a ten sleeper found under the house had the notation "London 1700" carved on it, so the timber is believed to have been salvaged from a ship. Free standing matching chimneys at either side of the house are made of English paving bricks on ballast stone foundations.

Several years ago, while exploring the possibility of installing an invisible heating system for the house, my son Michael, found a brick framework beneath the house, leading down into the ground. Mrs. Hellen Garner, a descendant of one of the early owners, says that what Mike found was the remains of a filled-in tunnel. This led either to the shore or into the woods for the purpose of smuggling goods into or out of the house, or for hiding from Indians or authorities. A trap door which is now covered over originally led from the house into the tunnel.

Many stories connect Blackbeard to Hammock House. He anchored his ship in the creek in front of

Pirates were a cantankerous bunch, often fighting
amongst themselves.

the house and tied his smaller boat up at one of the front porch pillars. Today that would be impossible. In Blackbeard's day, Taylor's Creek almost lapped at his front porch, but now it is several hundred yards away from the house. When a channel was dug in the creek, the spoils were used to fill in the marsh between the creek and Hammock House.

Blackbeard referred to Beaufort as "that poor little village at the upper end of the harbor."

He had been there previously with Hornigold, but in 1718, Blackbeard and Bonnet again visited Core Sound. At this time Blackbeard had four vessels with about 400 men, so his ships were over-crowded. He as the captain had his own cabin, but because of the crowded conditions, some of the men were forced to sleep on the open deck in bad weather.

For the first time there was serious dissension among the crews. Blackbeard was aggravated trying to control such a large group of unruly men who acted like school children, always squabbling over petty grievances. But what bothered him most was that the spoils had to be divided so many ways, leaving little for himself, when he wanted it all.

In June Blackbeard, under the pretense of careening the "Queen Anne," ran her aground, damaging the mainmast and some of the side planks. Then Blackbeard hollered to Israel Hands on the "Adventure," "Israel, get some men and help me pull my ship loose."

Israel Hands had been informed of Blackbeard's plans, so he threw lines from the nearest sloop as well as his own across the deck of the "Queen Anne." He made a great show of attempting to pull the ship free. While doing this, he further damaged the "Queen Anne's Revenge" and grounded the "Adventure." Both ships appeared to be damaged beyond repair.

Blackbeard had devised a devious plan to get rid of the men he didn't want and to avoid splitting his treasure so many ways. He told Bonnet, who was still more or less a prisoner, "I've just learned that King George has extended his offer of pardon to all pirates who will voluntarily seek clemency before September 5th. All that is required is to swear to forgo any further acts of piracy. I've decided to go to Bath Town and request a pardon from Governor Eden."

Bonnet listened eagerly. Blackbeard continued, "Since war is about to break out with Spain, I plan to apply for a commission as a privateer from King George. I'd advise you to do likewise."

Then as though an afterthought, "To do this you'll require a vessel. Would you like to have the 'Revenge' back?"

Do fish nibble at bait? Bonnet was so grateful he almost kissed Blackbeard. He should have known by now that Blackbeard had some devious plot in mind. But he didn't.

"When we get back, we'll divide up the spoils," Blackbeard promised. With someone as gullible as Bonnet, it almost took all the pleasure out of cheating him.

Bonnet left immediately by way of the inland waterways of Core and Pamlico Sounds for Bath Town. He took some of his original crew with him, leaving the remainder at Beaufort to repair the "Revenge."

When he arrived at Bath Town, Bonnet surrendered to Governor Eden and received his pardon and clearance papers for a voyage in the "Revenge" to St. Thomas' Island. He had barely left the governor's office when Blackbeard appeared.

When Bonnet returned to Old Topsail Inlet, he learned how Blackbeard had betrayed him. "Where has he gone?"

"He slipped out in a small boat in the dark of night and transferred everything of value from the other ships to the 'Adventure,'" his mate said.

Was there no end to Blackbeard's cupidity?

While trying to decide what to do next, Bonnet saw signals off in the distance on a desert island across the inlet. He sent several men in a long boat over to investigate. They soon returned with word that Blackbeard had marooned 17 men on a small sandy island without food or water or any means of obtaining any.

Even as Bonnet made arrangements to rescue the men, he was furious. "He took everything of value! He didn't even leave me with provisions or munitions. All I have is the 'Revenge" and more men than I can possibly use."

"That black hearted scoundrel! I'll see him dead."

Some of the men Bonnet rescued from the sand bar settled in the area rather than risk the hangman's noose that awaited them some place else. One is said to have made his way back to his home in New England and later returned to Carteret Precinct, where he became a man of some importance.

While staying at Hammock House, Blackbeard captured a French ship off Cape Lookout. Some claim he forced the passengers and crew to walk the plank. All except one 18 year old French girl whom he found comely. He threw her over his shoulder and carried her screaming into the house. And she never stopped screaming.

Apparently she didn't want to share his bed. On the next full moon he hanged her, still screaming, from a limb on a live oak tree in the back yard. Her body was buried beneath the tree before he went back out to sea.

Rumors flew that Blackbeard buried some of his treasure in the back yard too. Since then every inch has been dug up at least once trying to locate the loot. None was ever found.

The Hammock House, almost 280 years later, is still considered haunted. For many years, it stood neglected, paint peeling on the outside planks, weeds growing in the yard, deserted on a spit of land called Sandspur Hill. For a time gypsies camped down the path.

Then in 1982 the house sparkled with fresh white paint furnished for advertising purposes. The lawns were trimmed and green. But it is said that on nights when the moon is full, you can still hear the screams of a young girl whose ghostly body swings on a rope hanging from the limb of an old oak tree where Spanish moss sways in the wind.

THE HANGING OF STEDE BONNET

Bonnet was determined to take revenge upon that villain, Blackbeard. Since his men told him that Blackbeard had set sail for Ocracoke Inlet, he immediately set off to follow. But when he arrived, Blackbeard had already sailed a few hours earlier.

He had received his pardon and didn't want to return to piracy. He couldn't return to his old life at Barbadas, so he set sail for St. Thomas Island to obtain a pirvateer's license. After anchoring his vessel he proceeded ashore to the authorities. He wasn't concerned about leaving his ship in the care of his crew because he trusted them. It took longer than he had anticipated to complete the negotiations for the commission.

On his return even before boarding the "Revenge," he sensed something was wrong. No one was on the deck to hail him aboard. He searched the ship. No one was there. It was spooky being alone on his own sloop. Then he discovered not only was his crew missing, so were the foodstuffs and cargo he had purchased a few days previously from a small trading vessel.

When he saw some men on shore signaling to him, he poled over to pick them up. It proved to be three of his crew members.

"It were that scoundrel Blackbeard," the older

man said. "We figured he had brung us food and weapons, so we invited him to come aboard."

Then one of the others interrupted, "He pulled a gun on us and done stole our munitions and supplies. Then he took the crew prisoners. When he weren't looking, us'uns slipped over the side and swum ashore."

"What happened to the other men?" Bonnet asked.

"We don't know."

Bonnet, with his three remaining men, sailed slowly down the coast. He soon discovered the remainder of the crew on a deserted stretch of land. He anchored and sent his long boat over to rescue them. The words he used made even the most hardened of his men avoid contact with him.

Something had happened to Stede Bonnet. Two days later within sight of Cape Henry, when they sighted a sloop, instead of paying the captain for the supplies he needed, Bonnet took the cargo, put the crew ashore, and sank the ship. Stede Bonnet had returned to pirating.

When he had first encountered Blackbeard, he had been a joke, a gentleman pirate. Not any more. He was determined to be ruthless, even crueler than Blackbeard. As Blackbeard had learned how to be a pirate from Hornigold, so had Bonnet learned how to be one from Blackbeard. He had no sympathy for either prisoners or his men.

One day the quartermaster dragged two of his pirates before him. The men were so inebriated they could barely stand. "They broke open a barrel of rum and tried to drink it all."

"Throw buckets of sea water on them. Then strip them to the waist and tie them to the mast. Call all hands on deck to watch and give the thieves twenty lashes each."

When two men got into a fight with knives, Bonnet
ordered, "Maroon them on the next island we come
upon."

Bonnet is said to be the only pirate who ever
made prisoners "walk the plank." He acted with
such authority that his crew obeyed him without
protest.

Now that Bonnet was an all-out pirate, he changed
his name twice, finally settling on "Captain
Thomas." His sloop was no longer the "Revenge,"
it was the "Royal James." At this time Prince
James was plotting to overthrow the government
of George I to gain control of the throne of
England, so he named his ship after him.

It seemed the change of names was a success.
On his first cruise, he went as far north as
Delaware where he captured at least ten prizes,
containing a wealth of cargo. Two of these were
the "Frances" and the "Fortune."

But the "Royal James" had begun to leak. It
badly needed careening. With his two prize ships
in tow, he sailed south towards Cape Fear in North
Carolina.

The mouth of the Cape Fear was a rendezvous
for pirates. The myriad waterways offered
concealment. Besides this, North Carolina's
Governor Eden was gaining the reputation of being
soft on pirates.

When they had the "Royal James" careened on
its side, they discovered the bottom needed
extensive repairs.

Harriot, who was with Bonnet, suggested, "Why
don't we just take one of the prize ships and
junk this one?"

Bonnet looked at him like he was out of his
mind. "I purchased this vessel with my own funds.

We will repair it."
"What do you want to do? You know we can't go
into the city and buy the lumber we'll need."
"What do you suggest?"
"Break up one of the prize ships."
But these ships were valuable and in good
condition. "Be on the lookout for a stray vessel."
They found what they needed, a shallop. They
captured it and broke it up for lumber. They
lingered for two months.
This was a serious mistake. Word leaked out
that a pirate was laid up at the mouth of Cape
Fear. The governor was convinced it was Charles
Vane, the same pirate who had threatened to burn
Charles Towne. The people of South Carolina
(Charles Towne in particular) were fed up with
pirates. They knew they could not count on North
Carolina's Governor Eden or his secretary, Tobias
Knight, to take care of the North Carolina pirates.
So Governor Johnson of South Carolina vowed to
wipe out the pests if he could find the right
man to pursue them, even if he had to invade North
Carolina's territorial waters to accomplish this.
Colonel William Rhett, the receiver-general
of the colony, was the man he needed. He was given
command of the sloops, "Henry" and "Sea Nymph."
The two sloops sailed into the mouth of the Cape
Fear River, but since Rhett's men were not familiar
with the sandbars cluttering the mouth of the
river, they soon ran aground.
Aw--but through the trees, Rhett could see the
topmasts of a pirate ship. He realized high tide
wouldn't come until about midnight, so he knew
he wouldn't be able to re-float his sloops until
then.
It was almost sundown when one of Bonnet's

lookouts approached him. "We're not alone. I see the top masts of at least two vessels through the trees."

"Friend or foe?"

"Don't know."

"Take two men and go investigate. Be alert." He watched anxiously for their report. "It's two sloops. They're armed. Looks like big trouble."

He knew they couldn't be from Governor Eden, they had to be from South Carolina's Governor Johnson. Bonnet floated the "Royal James," abandoning the captured sloops. During the night, he wrote a letter to Governor Johnson, promising him if he survived the coming battle, he would plunder and burn every ship daring to leave Charles Towne.

When dawn came, Colonel Rhett attacked. Stede Bonnet was prepared. Muskets spit fire. Explosions shook both ships. Wood and pieces of sail were flying everywhere. Five hours later weary from fighting, the South Carolina crews were considering turning tail and returning to Charles Towne when the "Royal James" hoisted a white flag of surrender.

"What the devil...why are they surrendering? Is it a trick?" Rhett asked, not really expecting an answer from his navigator. "Those pirates aren't defeated. If he thinks Governor Johnson is going to be lenient with him, he's in for a big surprise."

Colonel Rhett was shocked when Stede Bonnet surrendered his ship, his men, and himself. When he met with the pirate captain to discuss surrender terms, his eyes widened, "You're not Captain Charles Vane."

"I never said I was." He made a slight bow. "You

have the honor of greeting Captain Stede Bonnet, the gentleman pirate, now known as Captain Thomas."

So this was that buffoon Blackbeard had taken under his protection.

During the battle, seven of the pirates had been killed and five wounded, two of whom later died of wounds. In Rhett's crew, ten or 12 of the men were killed, 18 wounded, several of whom later died of their wounds.

Stede Bonnet and his captured crew were taken on into Charles Towne. The crew was detained in a warehouse. But because Stede Bonnet, David Harriot, and Ignatius Pell were gentleman, they were placed in the custody of the marshal.

After Charles Vane had threatened to burn Charles Towne and Blackbeard had disgraced them by blockading the port, Governor Johnson had a vendetta against all pirates.

When Bonnet realized that Governor Johnson was preparing for a hanging, he knew he had made a serious mistake; this man was not going to be lenient. He had to get out of there. So he quickly made preparations to escape. The marshal for a few piles of silver not only allowed Bonnet and Harriot to escape, but he supplied them with a small sail boat with which to do it. Bonnet was wearing a dress when he fled.

Governor Johnson placed a reward on Bonnet's head. Colonel Rhett immediately pursued them. Harriot was killed and Bonnet recaptured.

At the trial of Bonnet's crew, Ignatius Pell turned traitor and testified against his crew mates. The only excuse the men offered in their own defense was that they had been forced into illegal acts of piracy by Stede Bonnet. All but four of the pirates were convicted and sentenced to be hanged.

On November 8, 1718, 29 members of the crew of the "Royal James" were hanged at White Point. As a lesson to all who might consider following in their footsteps, their bodies were left twisting in the wind for several days. Then they were buried in the mud flats somewhere between the high and low water marks. Soon the tide covered up their graves, leaving no evidence such men had ever existed.

Two days later, Stede Bonnet was brought to trial. When the charges against him were read, he answered, "Not guilty."

In his own defense he said, "I wouldn't have resorted to piracy if I had not been so desperate for funds." Snickers were heard in the courtroom. This was a ridiculous excuse, since it was well known he was wealthy.

Judge Trott said, "The sea was created by God for the use of man. It is susceptible to ownership and government like terra firma. The King of England enjoys sovereign rights over British waters. Commerce and navigation cannot dispense with laws. There have always existed special laws for the good ordinance of maritime affairs."

Then he reviewed a list of Bonnet's crimes. He thundered out the sentence, "Death by hanging!"

He condemned Bonnet to the tortures of Hell in "the lake which burneth with fire and brimstone, which is the second death." Trott roared that, "Surely this man will suffer the everlasting burnings."

Governor Johnson set December 10, 1718 as the date for Bonnet's execution. Bonnet, former pirate, now became a mere mewling coward of a man living out his last few days in terror.

Major Stede Bonnet was hanged on the gallows at
Charleston Court December 10, 1718. His body was
buried in the marsh below the low water mark.

He was confined to one small room. He wasn't
accustomed to being cramped into such a small
space. For months, the wide open seas had been
his home. Here all he could do was think. He
remembered his pampered childhood, his schooling,
his army career. His wife! God, how he remembered
his wife! For that nagging bitch he had given
up his sugar plantation, his friends, his life.
How could he have fallen so low? A man of his
background condemned to hang? He'd seen death
lots of times. He'd even killed his share. If
he'd been killed in battle, it would have been
more seemly. But to be hanged at the end of a
rope like a common thief? It was more than he
could bear. He couldn't sleep. He couldn't eat.
People were always watching. But he couldn't
hide his feelings. The last thing he wanted was
for people to pity him. But they did.

In spite of his past the sympathies of the
public, especially the women, flowed towards him.
A group of them petitioned the Governor to either
pardon him or else commute his sentence. Some
wanted him sent to England so his case could be
reviewed by the British government. Bonnet spent
most of his time writing letters. It was his only
chance for freedom. One of these was to Colonel
Rhett, the man who had twice captured him.

He was a seasoned soldier, but when Colonel
Rhett read the letter, tears came to his eyes.
He went to Governor Johnson. "If you will allow
me, Sir, I will take Bonnet to England for a second
trial."

"He's been tried. He's guilty. He hangs."

Bonnet himself wrote a letter to Governor
Johnson, claiming he had become a Christian,
pleading, "I implore you to spare me my life,

even if I have to cut off my arms and legs to obtain my pardon, leaving me only the use of my tongue with which to pray to God, to make penance every day and live clad in sackcloth and ashes."

Johnson ignored his plea.

The day of the execution dawned bright and sunny. Bonnet was almost in a state of collapse. He could hear voices outside laughing, talking, children playing, carrying on their ordinary lives. Didn't anyone realize that this was the day he was about to die?

Then he heard the creaking wheels of the hanging cart coming for him. Remembering their humiliation when Blackbeard had blockaded the town, everyone turned out to see this pirate die. Families poured in from the surrounding area. They brought their children to make a holiday of it. Hawkers sold food and drinks.

Instead of being taken directly to the place of execution, Bonnet was placed in a cart and taken around the city, so those who couldn't get close enough to view the event, could see this man who was about to die.

A little girl, in an act of compassion, pressed a small cluster of wildflowers in his manacled hands. When he was given the opportunity of speaking his few last words to the gaping crowd, no words would come. Then as the cart was pulled beneath the gallows, he mouthed the words, "Oh, my God, oh my God!"

He grasped the flowers tight in his hands. He heard the crack of a whip sending the cart ahead. This was it. He was "swung off" dangling by his neck.

Some cheered. Some boo-o-ed. Some wept.

His body was left hanging there four days before

it was buried at the edge of the marsh below the
water mark, near the graves of his comrades. The
gentle waves of the sea, which he had come to
love, have long since washed away all evidence
of his grave. And of his life.
 The gentleman pirate was now only a memory.

BATH TOWN WELCOMES THE PIRATES

In June of 1718, Blackbeard took the "Adventure" through the shallow Ocracoke Inlet, into Pamlico Sound, and up the Pamlico River to Bath Town. When Bath Town was made an official port, it was hoped it would become the commercial and political center of the colony.

In a sense it was successful, but it never quite attained the fulfillment expected. Merchants were buying and selling. The taverns were kept busy with sailors and local men. The ladies dressed in the latest fashions. It had a library, the first public library in the colony. It had no church building but services were held regularly in homes. The parish also established the first free school for Indians and blacks.

When Blackbeard sailed into Bath Town asking for his second pardon, ships from foreign countries were tied up at the docks, loading on naval stores, furs, and tobacco. He found the town busier and wealthier than either New Bern or Wilmington.

While those living on the Outer Banks and near Beaufort were poor, a few merchants and skilled artisans had settled in Bath Town. Planters and others came and bought lots, sometimes built houses, remained awhile, then moved on.

Most of the plunder taken from pirating along the North Carolina coast was taken into local ports and sold. The merchants were happy to see them come because they could purchase goods from them at reasonable prices. Planters and others flocked in from miles around to buy the foreign merchandise.

At Bath Town, Blackbeard swaggered up the street to the house where the governor lived.

Governor Eden greeted him warmly. He expected him. No one knows exactly what transpired between these two men. While Governor Eden consulted with his Council, the pirates paraded up and down the streets, bought grog in the taverns, and ignored bitter glares from some of the townsfolk.

Eventually Blackbeard and 20 of his men were awarded pardons. Once again, he was allowed to keep his ship. This time it was the "Adventure."He was awarded the goodies he had stolen. It has been suggested that the governor was pacified by being given a portion of the take, but this has never been proven.

The governor decided, "Since the vessel belonged to Spain, it is a legitimate prize." Everyone knew this was ridiculous—the ship was English.

So less than a month after his blockade of Charles Towne, Blackbeard was living the life of a wealthy gentleman in Bath Town. He purchased the house directly across from Governor Eden's on Back Creek. It is said that an underground tunnel led from the cellar of Eden's house to the base of a high cliff at the creek, enabling Blackbeard to transport illicit merchandise to Eden. If there was such a tunnel, it was built earlier as an escape route during Indian attacks.

While playing the gentleman at Bath, Blackbeard put aside the garments he wore while in battle and donned velvets and silks. His hat was clean and brushed, his shoes shined and buckles polished, his thick bushy eyebrows and beard carefully trimmed and groomed. His intense blue eyes twinkled, especially when he was trying to impress the ladies.

At his house, he entertained in a sumptuous fashion. The planters were welcomed into his home and he into theirs. He bought their friendship with gifts of rum and sugar. He bragged he could be invited into the finest homes in the land.

Whenever Blackbeard came into port any place, he found at least one "wench" irresistible. Some even claim that Blackbeard courted Governor Eden's daughter, but since she was already engaged to marry another young man, she rejected him. Blackbeard was so angered by this that he had her fiancee captured one night, chopped off his hands, killed him, and dumped the body into the sea. He placed the finance's severed hands in a jeweled case and had them delivered to Miss Eden. Imagine her horror when she opened the package! Heartbroken, she languished and died, as was the custom for heart-broken young ladies in those times.

Although this illustrates the cruelty of Blackbeard, there is no reason to believe the story is true. There is no record of Governor Eden having any children. He married a widow lady who had a son and a daughter.

Regarding Blackbeard's attraction to the ladies, the writer Doctor Charles Johnson states:

"He [Blackbeard] often diverted himself with going on shore among the planters, where he reveled night and day. By these he was well received, but whether out of love or fear, I cannot say. Sometimes he used them courteously enough, and

made them presents of rum and sugar, in recompense
of what he took from them; but as for liberties
which, 'tis said, he and his companions often
took with the wives and daughters of the planters,
I cannot take upon me to say whether he paid them
'ad valorem' or no."

Blackbeard liked the people of North Carolina,
and most of them liked him. He had the ability
to adjust to whatever situation he found himself.
But he realized the men who accompanied him were
not suitable to associate with his wealthy friends,
so he went alone.

While in Bath Town, Blackbeard found a 16 year
old daughter of a planter to his liking, and he
decided to marry her. Marriages had to be performed
by a minister or missionary if one was available.
If not then it was proper for the Governor or
one of his Council to perform the ceremony.

The Church of England was responsible for sending
out missionaries to tend to the spiritual needs
of her people. In 1717 and 1718, there were two
missionaries covering the area of Chowan and
Bath.

One was John Urmstone, a whining, ineffectual
man, who was constantly in debt. He claimed the
Vestry would not—or could not—pay him what was
due him. He felt he was entitled to a large house
and at least four servants. In a letter dated
May 2, 1718, he states:

"...I have been in Curratuck where I baptized
35 children and the Mother of one of them; she
hath 3 sisters and 2 Brethern all adults the sons
and daughters of an Anabaptist who pretends to
be a Physician Fortune Teller and Conjurer, always
chosen Burgess for that precinct and a leading

Blackbeard was a "lady's man." At every port he docked, there was at least one wench he found irresistible. While at Bath Town, he took a bride.

man in our Assemblies ...Many such as he who rather oppose than promote the Interest of our Church."

He said sometimes he would preach to only nine or ten and mentioned "riding five miles in vain, not to find a single soul there."

His financial condition became so severe that at the death of his wife, he stated he was sending his two youngest children to England "as a present to the Society, hoping they would place them in some charity school or hospital." He publicly disowned his oldest son. Also he insisted his bills had to be paid and several servants furnished.

Later an anonymous letter was received by the Society stating that Mr. Urmston's life "is wicked and scandalous. He is a notorious drunkard and swearing and lewdness is also what he is occupied of. For these and others of his vices he was so much disliked of the people he was among that scarce any of them come to hear him."

The other missionary was a Mr. Ebeneezer Taylor, an elderly gentleman who came up from South Carolina. He lived in a five room house, where he kept one large room in which to preach. In February of 1720, this same Mr. Taylor died off Harbor island while on a missionary journey to Beaufort. He was buried on Cedar Island. The governor had requested Mr. Urmstone make the journey, but since his wife was with child, he sent the old man in his place. In Beaufort there was no church building, but services were held in homes. An ordained minister was needed to perform baptisims and marraiges.

Mr. Urmstone could have officiated at the ceremony between Blackbeard (who was calling himself Teach again at this time) and the young girl, but apparently it was Governor Eden who read them their vows.

Some say that the bride was Mary Ormond, daughter of a planter. The name of Ormond later became an important one in Bath. If Blackbeard's bride gave birth to a child, it would have been given another last name to avoid the disgrace of having such a father.

It's strange that someone didn't inform the governor of Blackbeard's other wives, at least two in North Carolina besides the ten or so dusky brides in the West Indies. Or perhaps they did, and he chose to ignore them. If any of these marriages were legal, his marriage to the sixteen year old girl was bigamous.

If Blackbeard had thirteen or fourteen wives and was a pirate for only fifteen to eighteen months, he was a busy man. He was definitely a ladies' man. Wherever he went, the ladies tittered with excitement when he entered a room. His tall physique, his habit of treating them with loving concern won many a delicate heart. When the lucky (?) woman caught his eye, Blackbeard would get one of his men to perform a "wedding" ceremony.

He would bed her, sometimes with others watching, then turn her over to some of his crew for a few days until he left again, leaving his "wife" on shore. Some say he had a wife at Edenton and one at Elizabeth City as well as on the southern islands. It is not known how many children, if any, were born of these pseudo marriages.

Some families in eastern North Carolina claim they are descended from some of Blackbeard's marriages. An elderly lady who lived in Morehead City claimed Blackbeard married a Day woman and that the John Day family in Carteret County were descended from this marriage.

No one will ever know what was in Blackbeard's mind when he settled down at Bath Town, whether he intended to become a country gentleman, or whether he was up to his old tricks. But it seems that for awhile, he was satisfied.

But that small boy from Bristol had been thoroughly indoctrinated into his life as a sea robber. As it was when he was a child, he longed for the wide open seas, for adventure, for new places and new faces. He thought about his old mentor, Hornigold, who had retired, but still went about trying to capture other pirates. He understood the restlessness of an old sea dog on land.

Blackbeard attempted to keep his men under control, but they were not the sort to live peaceably on land. At sea they drank, gambled, and stole. On shore, they drank, gambled, whored, and stole. They were pirates. And they had not reformed.

Blackbeard decided to return to the sea.

The "Adventure" was licensed under the name of Captain Teach for trading expeditions on the high seas. Papers were cleared for a trading trip to St. Thomas.

Many of the citizens of Bath Town released a collective sigh of relief to see them leave. They appreciated the money and goods they brought but detested the men who brought them.

CRUISING THE COAST

If it is true, "There is a time for all things,"
then surely it was time for Blackbeard to leave
Bath Town.
His lavish style of living and entertaining
had drained his vast fortune, besides maintaining
the facade of a gentleman was tiring. In the
beginning, when he had first become "Blackbeard,
Terror of the Seas," it was an act. But now the
character he had created was so thoroughly
ingrained into his innermost being, appearing
as a gentlemen was the act.
He was surly and disagreeable. When his money
ran low, he was no longer welcome in the homes
of his wealthy acquaintances. These same neighbors
in whose homes he had been extravagantly
entertained now were robbed when the opportunity
presented itself. Ship captains coming up the
river complained of being hijacked. Blackbeard
and his men were suspected, but no one dared accuse
him to his face.
Blackbeard required more funds if he was to
keep up his affluent life style. So he sent out
word to the rest of his crew members who had come
with him to Bath Town to join him.
With no regrets, he left his young bride behind.
She was probably happy to see him go. He set
sail in the "Adventure," carrying with him his

certificate of ship registration and proof of
pardon of piracy. He told everyone he was going
on a trading expedition to the West Indies.

Back at sea Blackbeard was once again the
powerful, indomitable pirate on the prowl for
unwary prey. On his way south, he stopped three
English vessels, appropriated their stores and
other necessities, then allowed then to go on
their way.

Occasionally, he stopped off at plantations,
to provision his ship. He flirted at the edges
of Beaufort, Jacksonville, Wilmington, Charles
Towne, and Georgia. Sometimes he paid for what
he took, but too often he didn't.

When he became bored with cruising in the rivers
and inlets, he decided to return to Philadelphia
to visit with some of his old cronies. On his
trip north he probably stopped off at Edenton
and Elizabeth City. At Philadelphia it was like
being home again. He and his seamen walked boldly
up and down the streets, not even attempting to
hide.

Governor William Keith had been informed of
the pirates' arrival. In the Crown Colonies of
Virginia and Pennsylvania, their laws were more
strictly enforced than those of North Carolina.
They had prospered and were tired of being bothered
with pirates and were determined to erase piracy
from their shores.

Blackbeard was drinking and gambling with some
of his friends in one of his favorite taverns,
when one of his crew members rushed in. "The law
is coming. They got a warrant on us."

Blackbeard nonchalantly drained his tankard
of ale, wiped his beefy hand across his mouth,
then said, "It seems we've worn out our welcome

Blackbeard watches as two of his men dig a hole to bury treasure.

in this friendly town. Let's leave." Not willing to have a confrontation with the law, he prudently rounded up his crew and departed for Burmuda.

Since he had had no opportunity to provision, he robbed two English ships of what he needed, nothing else, then allowed them to sail on their way.

He met two French ships headed for Martinique. One was loaded with cocoa, sugar, spices, and other valuable merchandise. The other one was empty, carrying ballast. It was too much of a temptation to resist. He put both crews on the empty ship and sent them on their way. At this time England was not at war with France, so this was illegal.

Over the objections of some of his crew, he had the gall to sail up the Pamlico River to Bath Town with his stolen ship and cargo. He swaggered down the street to Governor Eden's residence, where he announced to a disbelieving Eden that he had "found the French ship at sea, not a soul aboard her."

He and several of his crew signed affidavits to that effect. Governor Eden convened a Vice-Admiralty Court with Tobias Knight as judge, condemning the French vessel as a legitimate privateering prize. Blackbeard was given permission to sell the cargo. He could also have legally sold the ship, but someone could have recognized it and caused trouble for him. Instead he had it declared as unseaworthy and received the governor's permission to destroy it. It was sailed up the river from Bath Town and set afire. The hull was then sunk to conceal the evidence.

Under the laws of salvage, 20 hogshead of sugar was awarded to Tobias Knight and 60 to Governor

Eden.

Blackbeard returned to sea, once again the merciless brute he had been before his pardon, plundering ships, anchoring at his favorite spot at Ocracoke, which he called Teach's Hole Channel.

Ocracoke Island is a part of the Outer Banks. It is also an Inlet and a village. He came to know all its coastline, its inlets and coves, where the best shelters were for his vessels.

From there, he went up and down the coast. He went into New Berne, where he reportedly stayed in a house on Front Street where the Thomas Sparrow House now stands. The original building was burned sometime between 1838 and 1842 when several fires destroyed that section of town near Union Point. The house which replaced it still stands.

At Ocracoke, for years there existed the crumbling foundation of a huge house. The older folks all said the house which was built there was called "Blackbeard's Castle." And that Blackbeard lived there while he was on shore. Here he counted his treasure and divided it among his men. The house had a turret where ships coming and going could be watched. If Blackbeard built the house, it was constructed from lumber taken from wrecked ships such as the "Queen Anne's Revenge."

On the night of September 14th, a planter by the name of William Bell with his young son and an Indian were anchored near John Chester's landing when he noticed a larger boat passing by, headed up river towards Tobias Knight's house.

An hour or so before dawn, this same boat came back down the river and stopped a few yards away. A man on board hailed him. "You got anything to drink?"

It appeared to Bell that there were five men on the boat to his three. He quickly decided he wanted nothing to do with them. "Because of darkness, I can't see who you are."

"All I want is a drink. Surely if you are a Christian man, you can spare me a drink. Or are you too good to drink with the likes of me?"

When Bell didn't answer, the man called to someone in his boat, "Hand me my sword."

"Be gone, you moth eaten maggot!" Bell shouted. He realized he was penned in between the intruder and the landing. There was no way he could escape.

The big man in the other boat jumped on his boat. "Put your hands behind your back, you lily livered scoundrel!"

But Bell wasn't about to surrender quietly. He grabbed the only weapon he had at hand, his knife, to defend himself. His assailant was strong, but his actions were awkward. The overpowering odor of rum explained why. But his weapon was longer and stronger than Bell's. The stranger beat him about the head with his sword until it broke off about a foot from the point.

William Bell dropped his knife and held his head with both hands, moaning. He surrendered.

The assailant demanded in a gruff voice, "Where are your pistols?"

Since Bell didn't want them to break into his strong box, he handed him the key. "At the bottom of the chest, beneath the ledger." Bell with his son and Indian were left at the landing while his boat was taken farther out into the river. The thieves took everything of value, then threw the oars and sails overboard and sailed on down the river.

It took two hours for Bell and his son to make

their way by land several miles up river to Governor Eden's house where he reported the theft.

He was referred to Tobias Knight, the Chief Justice. "I was robbed. It were that Edward Teach," he declared. "He had some men with him who was either black or else blacked to look like Negroes."

But Tobias Knight said, "My dear man, surely you are mistaken. I have it on good authority that Edward Teach is nowhere near Bath Town at this time."

"I know it were him. I want to swear out a warrant against Teach."

"Impossible. You cannot swear out a warrant against a man who wasn't even here." Knight calmly lit his pipe. "If you insist on a warrant, it will have to be against an unnamed person." He filled out the document and pointed out the place for Bell to sign.

Bell realized he would not get any satisfaction from this man and signed his "X" to the document, knowing it was pointless.

FESTIVAL AT OCRACOKE

Near the end of September, 1718, Blackbeard was anchored at Teach's Hole Channel, when several large ships approached. Through his spyglass, he picked out a large brigantine and several smaller ships.

"It's Members of the Brethern." Life had become boring and he longed for the companionship of the other pirates.

Hauling anchor, he sailed out into the inlet, where he welcomed his guests with a barrage of cannon fire.

Captain Charles Vane, commander of the fleet, replied with a salute from his guns. Vane was the most important "wanted" pirate loose on the seas at that time. Since he had refused the King's pardon at New Providence and had later harassed Charles Towne, South Carolina's Governor Johnson had sworn to capture him. He was the one Governor Johnson had hired Colonel Rhett to catch in the incident on the Cape Fear River, when he had found and captured Stede Bonnet instead.

Later Jack Rackham ousted Charles Vane as Captain because Vane refused to fight a large, well armed ship. Vane was marooned on an island, rescued by a supposed friend, who turned him over to the authorities.

Doctor Charles Johnson described the festival

82

Blackbeard entertained visiting pirates at a
festival at Ocracoke.

which followed as the largest pirate gathering ever to take place on the mainland of North America.

Blackbeard was once again in his element. "Men break out the rum. Prepare a feast. Our friends need wined and dined." He went among his guests and hugged his comrades.

Among the celebrities present were Charles Vane, Robert Deal, and Jack Rackham (called Calico Jack because of the calico pants he wore). Since Anne Bonny and Mary Read were on a vessel with Calico Jack Rackham in Charles Vane's flotilla, they were probably part of the crowd.

Anne Bonny and Mary Read were two of the most ferocious of pirates. Anne was born in Ireland, the daughter of a prominent lawyer and his maid servant. Her father's name was William Cormac. The scandal of his affair ruined his reputation and his law practice. He immigrated to South Carolina, leaving behind his wife, taking with him his maid who passed as his wife, and their child, Anne. At first he practiced law, then became a merchant and bought a plantation near Charles Towne. Soon after their arrival in America, Anne's mother died.

Anne grew up as a red-haired, freckle-faced Tom boy, following her stern, masculine father about the plantation. Even when she was a young girl she tried to run the household. She learned to ride like an Indian, shoot accurately, and handle a sword as if she were a boy. Another Indian trick she became adept at was knife throwing. Anne's hot temper matched her red hair, often getting her into trouble.

One day towards evening she ordered a house servant, "Prepare roast duck for supper." This would take hours and supper was already prepared.

"I take my orders from the housekeeper, not from the likes of you," the servant wriggled her ample bottom in contempt.

Anne's fierce temper flared. "How dare you speak thus to me!" Before she realized what she was doing, she hurled her knife at the slave. The slave slumped to the floor, soon dead in a pool of her own blood.

Anne was 16 before her father became concerned about his wayward daughter. Tucking her flaming red hair back with a cap and wearing boy's clothing she had begun to hang around the waterfront, listening to the tales of pirating told by the old seamen. It was here she met Jim Bonney, an ambitious pirate serving as mate on Stede Bonnet's pirate ship, "Revenge."

When Anne's father found them together, he snarled, "If you insist on seeing this penniless seaman, you are no longer my daughter."

"So?" Anne packed a few boy's clothes and a food hamper. She stole her father's dueling pistols and slipping her sheath knife in her belt, met Jim in a waterfront tavern. They convinced a nearby minister that Anne was pregnant so he would marry them. They honeymooned on a wooded hill high above the river, while they waited for the "Revenge" to arrive.

Anne brazenly told Captain Stede Bonnet that she was a runaway bond servant. Outwardly he accepted her story, but secretly he wondered if perhaps the young "man" was romantically involved with Jim Bonney.

The pirate ship encountered several merchant vessels, boarded and captured them, setting the luckless passengers ashore on an island. Then

they made their way to the West Indies, where
they rendezvoused with the famous pirates of that
day.

While there, they discovered that when he
arrived, the new governor, Woodes Rogers, would
be offering amnesty to any pirates promising to
forgo pirating.

"I'm going to accept his offer. I'll make a
fortune telling him what I know about the Brethren
of the Coast," Jim Bonny boasted.

Anne had already learned that the man was she
married to was insanely jealous. Now she found
his ratting on his former companions to be
contemptible. Anne was fond of both money and
men. She began to bestow her affections
indiscriminately on other men.

When Bonny discovered Anne in a compromising
position with a dashing young pirate lieutenant,
Jack Rackham, he yanked her away from him.

Anne slapped Bonny's face. "You're contemptible.
I'm going to marry Jack."

"You're my wife," Bonny said. "You're going
with me to New Providence."

Rackham had evidenced no shame at being caught
with another man's wife. Instead he offered,
"I'll buy her from you. How much do you want to
divorce her?"

"My wife is not for sale." If a man had made
such a proposal to most men, he would have been
either beat up immediately or else challenged
to a duel.

But not Jim Bonny. He attempted to pull her
away from Rackham, but she wouldn't move. "You're
my woman. If you don't come with me, I'll tell
the governor you've been unfaithful and have you
publicly flogged, you whore!" Bonny set off to

Anne Bonny may have looked like an angel, but in battle, she fought as fiercely as any man in the crew.

do as he threatened.

So to avoid the law Anne took off with Rackham. She became the newest member of Charles Vane's crew. Anne adored her pirate. In his book Doctor Johnson tells of one time when a young crewman made advances towards her, she attacked him and beat him so badly no one else dared come near her.

That is until a new member of the crew made friends with her. Rackham became jealous when he saw them walking arm in arm together.

Rackham drew his dagger,"Tell me why I shouldn't slit your throat." He drew it across the young pirate's neck.

Anne grabbed his arm. "Don't kill him. Let him go."

"Why should I"

"Because..." Anne ripped the young man's shirt down the front.

"Captain, I'm no threat to you," the young pirate said. Her full white breasts spilled out. She cupped them in her hands and held them out to him.

"Wh-ho are you?" Rackham sputtered.

"My name is Mary Read. When my husband died, I decided to become a pirate." Mary was of a rather short, stocky build, masculine in appearance.

Anne had become enamored of Mary before she knew she was female. Some say Mary Read was born in England. Others claim she was born in North Carolina of a woman who was burned as a witch. Her past was colorful, including a hitch in the English army where she passed as a man, wearing the regular uniform.

After Rackham discovered her sex, since she had proven herself as a pirate, she was allowed to remain on the ship. Anne and Mary became the best of friends, wearing expensive, low-cut gowns obtained in the pirate loot. On shore they put aside their pretense of being men. On board ship, they changed to men's clothing when a prize was sighted. Mary found love and married an impressed seaman on board the vessel. She saved his life by taking his place in a duel.

Both Mary and Anne were of a violent nature and in battle were as blood thirsty and cruel as the rest of the crew.

When Anne discovered she was pregnant, they sailed for Cuba where many of the families of the pirates made their homes while their husbands and fathers were at sea. Anne remained on shore only long enough to deliver her child, then left the baby with another family and went back out to sea.

During October of 1720 Rackham's ship, "Curlew," was attacked by an armed British sloop. Anne and Mary with the aid of one seaman fought off the enemy while Rackham and his men cowered below deck.

"Come on out and fight, you yellow-bellied cowards!" Anne shouted at Rackham and his men.

The women put up a good fight but were subdued. One of the marines said, "I couldn't kill a woman."

Later when they were sentenced to die, both women said, "We plead our bellies." This proved to be true, so the hanging was postponed. Mary's husband was released since he had not voluntarily joined the pirates. Rackham was sentenced to be hanged.

Before he was executed, Anne was given an opportunity to speak to him. "I'm sorry to see this happen,"she said. "But if you had fought like a man you wouldn't be hanged like a dog."

Mary became ill and died. Anne was unexpectedly pardoned.

One or both of these women were probably present at the festival at Ocracoke.

It soon became known pirates were anchored there, and fishermen and traders converged on the ships, bringing cattle, hogs, and fresh vegetables and fruits for trade. As long as Blackbeard was there, no one feared the pirates. Numerous hogs and cows were butchered and barbecued. The punch bowls overflowed with rum. Some men had instruments and they sang and danced. Some hunted and fished. It was one continuous party. They exchanged the latest news. Vane and Rackham brought word from the West Indies, and Blackbeard news from Pennsylvania and North Carolina. Finally the time came for Captain Vane and his fleet to depart.

As Blackbeard watched the last sail fade over the horizon, a tear came to his eye. He felt as if he was saying goodbye to his family.

Word of the drunken festival reached the ears of Governor Spotswood of Virginia. He feared that the pirates were planning to establish a pirate's fortress at Ocracoke. He was told Blackbeard planned to make it into a haven, a refuge for pirates with himself as King, charging every ship wanting to pass through a certain percentage of prize money.

Governor Spotswood immediately set about making plans to put an end to this threat. Ocracoke Inlet wasn't many hours away by water. If this story was true and Blackbeard built a pirate fortress in North Carolina, no vessels would be safe in either North Carolina or Virginia waters.

90

VIRGINIA DECIDES TO ACT

The inhabitants of the Crown Colony of Virginia believed they were superior to those living in that upstart Proprietary Colony of North Carolina to the south. Virginia had prospered while North Carolina remained the poor relative. And as those of wealth fear relatives with less possessions and funds taking advantage of them, so did Virginia.

In fact it is believed the Virginia authorities were making vague plans to buy out the Lord Proprietors and annex the North Carolina territory to Virginia. They disputed the boundary line between the two colonies. And Virginia objected to North Carolina's shipment of tobacco to Virginia. They even went so far as to discourage immigrants from settling in North Carolina.

The situation came to a head in 1717 when, because of pirates' interference, shipping in Chesapeake Bay came almost to a standstill.

While the Colony of North Carolina was impoverished, piracy was flourishing. When word came to Governor Spotswood that pirates had plans to settle permanently on the North Carolina Outer Banks, he was determined to put a halt to it. But he was having his own political problems. He lived in a sumptous house, almost a castle in Williamsburg. His extravagant life style was causing some to speak of impeachment. Ridding his own colony and that ragged colony to the south of pirates would greatly increase his own image.

Although he probably wouldn't admit it to himself, in many ways he was similar to Blackbeard. They were both ambitious for power and wealth. They loved adventure and their reputations were of utmost importance to them. It has been suggested Spotswood was jealous of Blackbeard. That thieving pirate was receiving the attention he should have been getting. This wasn't fair.

Spotswood consulted with one of his Council, "How can we legally get this man, Blackbeard?"

"Well, since he has been pardoned, in order to arrest him, proof of piracy after his pardon must be obtained."

"I have contacts in Carolina. Let me see what I can do."

He soon discovered that Governor Eden had his enemies. All men in authority did. He was given the names of Colonel Maurice Moore and Edward Mosely, both men of considerable importance in the colony. Contacts were made. A delegation arrived from North Carolina begging for his help in ridding them of the pirates. They brought with them affidavits, signed by some of the leading citizens, testifying to the close relationship of Governor Eden to Blackbeard.

"That's not enough," the Councilman said. "We need evidence of ships captured before we can act."

Former pirates had begun to be seen in the taverns and around the docks of Virginia's coast. "They're infiltrating the colony," Spotswood complained.

"Some of them are originally from here and

just came home," his aide said.

Spies reported to Spotswood, "William Howard is down at the tavern drinking. I know he was from here, but didn't he travel with Blackbeard?"

"Right. I think he was Blackbeard's quartermaster not long ago," Spotswood said. "Was he alone?"

"Yes, except for two Negroes. I heard him bragging about taking one from a French ship and the other one from a British vessel."

"If he took one from a British vessel, that's piracy."

Spotswood began to plot how he could use Howard to learn more about Blackbeard--where he anchored, his strength, and his plans. He issued a warrant for William Howard and his two Negroes. The money Howard had on him when he was arrested was confiscated.

This was good, but it didn't prove anything. "Find something to charge Howard with," Spotswood ordered.

They claimed he was insolent and indigent, but instead of legally arresting him and bringing him to trial, he was shipped aboard the British man-of-war, "Pearl," as a seaman. This vessel was under the command of Captain George Gordon and Lieutenant Robert Maynard.

At this time, even though the colonies had no legal right to try pirates, most governors ignored this and tried them by a commission of judges or trial by juries.

Because of the intervention of Commissioner John Holloway, after considerable legal wrangling, it was decided Howard was being held on board the "Pearl" illegally. Therefore, he was brought back to be given a "fair" trial.

Governor Spotswood found a loophole in the law, allowing him to try Howard without grand or petit juries. In a previous pirate trial in Virginia, both juries had been utilized, and in South Carolina the trial of Stede Bonnet was held by both such juries.

Howard was transferred to the public jail at Williamsburg awaiting trial before a Court of Vice-Admiralty on charges of piracy.

Captains Ellis Brand and George Gordon, commanders of British man-of-wars in Chesapeake Bay and Commissioner John Holloway were appointed to sit as judges. But because Holloway had previously been hired by Howard, he was removed from the case. He was replaced by Virginia's Attorney General John Clayton.

Howard was charged with serving, "...one Edward Tach and other Wicked and dissolute Persons..." and not having the "Fear of God before his Eye nor Regarding the Allegiancey due to his Majesty nor the just Obedience he ow'd to the Laws of the Land..."

It was a prejudiced court. With two naval officers and the Attorney General as judges, there was no doubt in either Governor Spotswood's or William Howard's minds as to the outcome of the trial.

Under questioning Howard broke down, "Yes, it's true. Blackbeard did go back to pirating after his pardon."

"How many ships has he captured since then?"

"I only know of two."

The verdict was, "Guilty of piracy. William Howard, you are sentenced to he hanged by the neck until you are dead."

But luckily for him, in true dramatic fashion,

the night before he was to be hanged, the warden
came to him. "A reprieve has arrived in the form
of a missive from London. All acts of piracy
committed before July 23, 1718 have been pardoned."

Since it could not be proved that Howard had
been actively pirating since that date, he was
released.

Whether or not Howard was hanged was of little
importance to Spotswood. While he was incarcerated
Howard had given the information concerning
Blackbeard that Spotswood needed.

He studied the map spread before him on his
desk and located Ocracoke Inlet. "This is the
place. It leads to Bath Town and to Blackbeard.
Now all we have to do is to figure out the best
way to capture him without him discovering our
plans."

PLANNED ATTACK

Virginia's Governor Spotswood was determined that Blackbeard, Bristol's blight upon North America's coastal shipping, would be eliminated. Any excuse would do. Some later questioned the authenticity of requests for intervention against him from the citizens of North Carolina. It wasn't an official request or even from the majority of the residents. Certainly Governor Eden authorized no such request.

Except from those he robbed, most of the citizens tolerated the pirates and traded with them.

William Bell and the others Blackbeard had robbed would be pleased if someone put him permanently out of business.

Britain had furnished Virginia with two man-of-war Royal Navy ships for their protection; the "Pearl," commanded by Captain Gordon and the "Lyme," commanded by Captain Brand. They had been stationed in the James River, patrolling the shore for about ten months. So far they had not seen any real action, but their presence made the citizens feel safe and was a deterrent to the pirates.

Being of the Royal Navy, they were not under the direct command of the governor but generally followed his instructions.

Spotswood deliberately spread the rumor that Blackbeard was fortifying Ocracoke as a pirate hangout. He consulted with the naval captains, suggesting they cruise along North Carolina shores and see if they could catch the man.

"When you see him use those cannon to blast him off the face of the earth!"

They were unsuccessful. "Sorry, Governor. Every time we spot that bastard, he ducks into an inlet or into water so shallow we can't follow."

Of course they couldn't catch him. The war ships, especially carrying heavy cannon, were too cumbersome and drew too much water to navigate the inlets of North Carolina's Outer Banks.

Governor Spotswood decided on a two-pronged attack on Blackbeard, one by land and one by sea. Because he wanted to use the element of surprise, he did not ask the Virginia Legislature to finance the expedition.

Instead, Governor Spotswood leased two sloops with his own funds, the "Ranger" and the "Jane." It has been speculated the reason he financed the expedition was a selfish one, he hoped to acquire some of Blackbeard's fabulous wealth which was believed to be hidden either on his ship or buried somewhere near Bath Town.

He placed Captain Brand in overall command. Brand was to lead a land expedition to Bath Town where Blackbeard owned a house. Lieutenant Robert Maynard with the "Jane" and "Ranger" was to go by sea. They hoped to box Blackbeard in with this maneuver. Captain Gordon was to remain with the Naval vessels to take care of any possibility of attack in Virginia.

Because Maynard wanted trained fighting men for his campaign, he chose 60 marines and sailors from the naval ships. They were furnished with small arms and sufficient ammunition, but in order

to keep the vessels light, they would carry no
cannon. Two pilots, who claimed to be familiar
with North Carolina coastal waters, were hired
as guides.

Realizing that the men might not want to risk
their lives unless there were to be rich rewards,
he promised that the Assembly of Virginia would
offer a reward of 100 pounds for those responsible
for the capture of Blackbeard and his pirates
within one year's time.

Spotswood was facing opposition from his own
council, a government crises. Efforts were underway
in the Virginia Legislature to have him impeached.
They objected to his extravagant life style and
an extensive land grant which somehow ended up
in his name. He needed a new project to restore
confidence to his regime. Capturing the pirate
Blackbeard would provide this encouragement.

At three o'clock on the afternoon of November
17, 1718, the two leased sloops lifted anchor
and slipped out of what is now Hampton, Virginia,
headed for Blackbeard's North Carolina hideout.
They traveled slowly in order for the land force
to arrive at the same time.

From vessels traveling northward, they learned
of Blackbeard's exact location, not at Bath Town,
but at Ocracoke Inlet. They allowed no vessels
to pass them going towards Ocracoke to warn the
pirates of their coming.

Captain Brand and his party left for Bath Town
the night of November 17. On November 22nd, they
arrived at Albemarle Sound, where they were met
by two of Governor Eden's political enemies,
Colonel Maurice Moore, and Colonel Edward Mosely.
These men assisted Brand and his men and horses
across the sound.

Since Brand represented the King, they found no opposition from the residents they met along the way. At ten o'clock, the night of November 23rd, they came within sight of Bath Town. Brand told Moore, "Go on into town. Find out if Blackbeard is there."

Within a short time, Moore returned. "He's not there now. But he's expected soon."

Brand proceeded to the home of Governor Eden at his Thistleworth plantation. Eden's welcome was polite but restrained. "And why am I honored by the presence of the Crown's representative in my home?"

"I am searching for that blackguard, Blackbeard. I have received word he is located in this area."

Eden called Tobias Knight in from the outer office. "Is Edward Teach in town?"

Knight returned in a few minutes. "I'm told he is expected at any time."

"And why do you want Edward Teach?" Eden was sarcastic, using the name he preferred for the pirate.

"For piracy."

"Are you not aware he has been pardoned?"

Brand's lip curled in disdain, but he swallowed, then presented Governor Eden with a letter from Governor Spotswood. "This document will explain."

"You can tell your Governor Spotswood that since his pardon, Mr. Teach has been trading up and down the Pamlico and Neuse Rivers. He cannot be prosecuted for past crimes."

Since they could not locate Blackbeard and had no word from Lieutenant Maynard, Brand on November 24th, sent two canoes down the Pamlico River in search of Maynard and his sloops.

They returned saying that Blackbeard was at

Ocracoke Inlet engaged in battle with Maynard and the British Navy.

At this time, Blackbeard had only a skeleton crew--about 18 men, few of whom were skilled fighters. The arrival of Lieutenant Maynard with two armed sloops was not exactly a surprise to Blackbeard. Tobias Knight, Governor Eden's Secretary and Collector of Customs, had spies in Virginia. He had sent a memo alerting Blackbeard of a possible attack. Blackbeard didn't take this warning seriously; he had heeded such rumors before and been disappointed when nothing happened.

Didn't they know he was Blackbeard, Terror of the Seas? He feared no man, not even Satan Himself. He spent the night drinking with the captain and three crewmen from a trading vessel anchored nearby.

During the carousals of that night, one of his men asked, "In case anything should happen to you during the engagement on the morrow, does your wife know where your treasure is buried?"

He replied, "Nobody but myself and the Devil know where it is. And the longest liver shall take it all."

Some say Blackbeard was so drunk his men tied him to the mast, lest he should fall overboard.

Others say Blackbeard spent the entire night pacing up and down the deck, waiting for the cock to crow at dawn when the attack would come. That Ocracoke got its name, from Blackbeard repeating, "O crow cock! Oh, crow cock!"

Actually the name was older than this. It probably evolved from the Indian name "Wokokin."

Lieutenant Maynard received word that two masts of a sloop could be seen over the sand dunes. He sent out a cutter with a reconnaissance party.

It returned. "It's Blackbeard."

So Maynard spent the remainder of the night making final preparations for the morning attack. Since the two pilots he had hired were uncertain of the channel, at dawn Maynard sent out a rowboat ahead of the sloops to lead the way through the shallow waters.

As the sky in the east began to lighten, one of Blackbeard's men untied him from the post and tried to wake him. "A ship is approaching!"

"Clear out and go sleep off your drunk. That's what I intend to do." But through the morning light, he could see a row boat followed by a sailing vessel heading towards him. "Damn. This is one time I should have listened to Knight's warning."

It was true—the English were about to attack. But he was Blackbeard, King of the Pirates. He wasn't worried. This was what he had been preparing for ever since he left Bristol. He mustered his men, distributed arms, loaded his cannon, then waited. But he was never one to waste time waiting for the enemy to come to him. He gave the orders, "Cast off the moorings."

The English bore down on the "Adventure," but Blackbeard was an excellent navigator, making the best use of current and wind, out-sailing Maynard.

Maynard watched anxiously. "What is he trying to do? We can't allow him to escape!"

"He's slowing down," his second in command said. "He's run aground!"

"Could be a trick," Maynard was doubtful. "But continue to advance and stand to."

When they were within hailing distance, he could hear Blackbeard swearing and hurling insults.

Maynard was about to open fire. Then he shouted, "By God, he's turned. He's headed towards us!"

THE BATTLE BETWEEN THE CROWN AND SATAN

Maynard hoisted the Union Jack and headed towards the tip of Ocracoke Island and the waters of the sound.

Blackbeard surprised both his men and the English by shifting directions and heading directly toward shore. The "Jane"and the" Ranger" followed, unaware they were being led into a trap. Soon they were grounded by the narrow channel and dangerous shoals. So was the "Adventure." Maynard shouted to his men, "Lighten the ship!" Men threw the ballast and water overboard. The "Jane" floated free. Utilizing every sail and oar, they came at Blackbeard.

Blackbeard hailed him from across the water, "Damn you for villains, who are you and from whence come you?"

Lieutenant Maynard answered, "You can see from our colors we are no pirates."

Blackbeard said, "Send your boat over so I may see who you are."

"I cannot spare my boat, but I will come on board of you as soon as I can with my sloop," Maynard boldly answered.

Blackbeard seized a bowl of liquor, guzzled liberally, then toasted his enemy, saying, "Damnation seize my soul if I give you mercy or take any from you."

Maynard replied, "I shall expect no quarter from you nor will I give any."

With this, Blackbeard's "black Ensign with the skeleton on it was run up the mast head.

While they were shouting at each other, the pirate's ship floated. Blackbeard signaled for his men to fire. The sloops were advancing towards them. The pirates fired broadside, charged with all manner of small shot. Four shots struck the "Jane," and several crewmen were hit. On the "Ranger" many men were either killed or wounded, including the master.

Maynard returned fire, shooting away the "Adventure's" forehalliards, and like the attacking vessel, it was now unmanageable. It drifted towards the "Jane." Leaving the dead bodies on the bloody deck, Maynard ordered his men, "Everyone except the man at the helm, hide below. Take your pistols, cutlasses, and swords. Be prepared to act when I call. Let him think we are almost unattended."

They drifted closer to the pirate ship. "If the pirate wants to fight, let him come to us."

As the two ships drew closer together, Blackbeard threw "grenadoes" made of case-boxes and filled with powder, small shot, slugs, and pieces of lead and iron, with a quick-match in the mouth of them, onto the enemy deck. Loud explosions shook the ship. A dense cloud of smoke arose, turning day into night.

Had not the English crew been under cover, damage would have been disastrous.

Blackbeard cried out to his men, "They are all knocked on the head except three or four. Board her and cut them to pieces."

As the smoke from the grenade cleared, Maynard could see the imposing figure of Blackbeard.

He looked exactly like he had expected. Smoke
swirled around his evil head. He was brandishing
a cutlass. Long pistols hung from a broad leather
strap across his massive chest.

He glared at Maynard.

Maynard thought truly he was looking into the
evil eye of Satan himself. A lesser man would
have turned and fled. But Maynard was resolute.
It would be a battle to the end. Would be to God,
that good would triumph.

Ten yards, five yards—Blackbeard's men quickly
surrounded their leader and master, as resolute
as their enemies. They realized that if they were
captured, they would dangle at the end of a
hangman's noose. The pirates threw grappling irons
across the bulwarks of the "Jane."

Seeing no one on board the English sloop,
Blackbeard thought that his grenades had killed
or wounded the last of them except for Maynard.
He would show this English upstart who he was.

As soon as the two sloops were joined, Blackbeard
leapt across the interval. The two captains met
face to face. At the same instant, both men fired
their pistols. Blackbeard missed (probably as
a result of all that drinking the night before).
But a ball from Maynard's gun ploughed into the
pirate's body.

Instead of falling, Blackbeard attacked Maynard.
As pirates scrambled over the gunwales, men poured
up from the hold. Hand to hand combat ensued.
Trained Englishmen were prepared to fight to the
death. So were the pirates.

Blackbeard didn't hesitate. Brandishing his
cutlass, he dealt blows left and right, striking
down those despised English, his own countrymen.
He was once again in his element. He was no longer

a man; he was evil incarnate. Bullets whistled near his ears, drowning out the cries of wounded men.

Blackbeard exalted in the role he had created for himself—his last appearance as Blackbeard, Terror of the Seas.

In the beginning the advantage lay with the pirate. In the course of hand-to-hand fighting, Blackbeard's heavier sword was wielded with such strength, that Maynard's sword was shattered at the hilt.

Blackbeard hurled himself at Maynard swinging his cutlass, pressing in for the kill. All Maynard could do was to hurl the hilt of his broken sword at him. At precisely the same moment a sailor raised his sword with both arms and delivered a powerful blow to the nape of the neck and throat of Blackbeard. Blood spurted like a fountain. Instead of Blackbeard's cutlass striking Maynard's neck, it was deflected and struck his hand.

Blackbeard staggered, clearly wounded. A lesser man would have toppled over dead. But not Blackbeard. Already wounded many times, he continued to fight like a wounded steer. He attacked Maynard, who by this time had seized another cutlass. Maynard attempted to deliver the pirate the final blow.

Blackbeard, already bleeding like a sieve from cutlass and pistol wounds, knocked out several assailants while trying to get at Maynard. Treading on the dead and wounded, Blackbeard with his back to the mast, continued to fight, his clothes in tatters, not seeming to feel his wounds.

The battle continued, Maynard with 12 men and Blackbeard with 14. The sea swirled with blood as red as burgundy wine all around the vessel.

Blackbeard (Edward Teach) fought Lieutenant Robert Maynard of the British Navy at Ocracoke Inlet on November 22, 1718.

Bravery was shown on all sides.

Even though Blackbeard had been wounded by the first shot from Maynard and had received 20 cuts and many more shots since then, he continued to fight.

But eventually, as he was in the act of cocking his pistol, he fell with a mighty thump on the deck. The pirate who embodied the evil of all pirates was dead. Only his legend lingers on, immortal.

AFTER THE BATTLE

The writer, Dr, Johnson, states that when the living crew members saw Blackbeard fall dead, they realized the end had come. He says, "all of the rest, much wounded, jumped overboard and called out for quarter, which was granted; though it was only prolonging their lives for a few days."

Near the end of the battle, the "Ranger" had advanced and attacked the few pirates remaining on the "Adventure." By mistake, in "friendly fire" one of the Royal Navy accidentally shot one of his own comrades.

In the hold of the Adventure, Blackbeard had posted his old friend, the huge Negro named Caesar, with orders to blow up the ship if the Navy should be victorious. When Caesar learned that his master was dead, he attempted to carry out his final orders.

But he was not alone. Also in the hold were two crew members from the trading vessel who had been drinking with their captain and Blackbeard the previous night. They had remained hidden in the hold throughout the action. Now they overpowered Caesar and prevented him from blowing up the ship.

There is some dispute about the number of pirates and sailors who were killed or who later died from wounds, but probably nine pirates were dead along with their master. Nine pirates were living, but all of them were wounded. Of Maynard's crew ten were killed and 24 were wounded, one of whom died later.

While searching through Blackbeard's belongings, they discovered a number of letters, several from leading New York merchants. Another letter began, "My Friend," and was signed "T Knight." This letter contained a lightly veiled warning and indicated that Governor Eden would welcome a visit from Blackbeard. Maynard also discovered an account book which contained information concerning the disposal of loot taken by the pirate.

Maynard took these items with him as proof of Blackbeard's activities.

Returning to the deck, he ordered Blackbeard's head severed from his huge body. Then it was hung beneath the bowsprit of the sloop. His shot riddled, slash wounded body was tossed overboard.

The surviving pirates swore that Blackbeard's body swam several times around the ship searching for its head, before it finally sank.

Maynard then sailed with the pirate's head swinging from the bowsprit to Bath Town to report to Brand, who was in charge of the expedition, and to obtain medical aid for his wounded men.

When Maynard arrived in Bath Town, Colonel Moore and Colonel Mosley reported that some of the loot was hidden in the governor's barn. They found the sixty hogsheads of sugar belonging to the governor and twenty belonging to Tobias Knight.

From Blackbeard's vessel and from the warehouse, Maynard confiscated goods worth more than 2,000 pounds were found in a barn. These goods were the

Lieutenant Maynard had Blackbeard's head cut off
and hung it from the bowsprtit of his ship, where
birds plucked out his evil eyes.

property of North Carolina, not Virginia.

The people of Bath Town watched as Maynard and his men paraded up and down the streets. Some mourned the loss of Blackbeard. He had brought the town to life. His occasional presence and the cheap merchandise he brought had been more than welcome. Had Maynard required assistance from the citizenry, in spite of the pirates' gross behavior, it is doubtful he would have received it. If the public had to choose between the two men; Maynard or Blackbeard, they would have voted overwhelmingly for the pirate.

After his men had been healed, Maynard proceeded on to Virginia, his grisly trophy still displayed from the bowsprit.

In Virginia, they were joyfully welcomed.

The prisoners were brought to trial by a court convened by Governor Spotswood. All but two of the pirates were condemned to die. One of these had been taken from a trading vessel the day before the battle. He had received more than seventy wounds which now had healed. He was released.

The other one was Israel Hands. He had not taken part in the battle because he was in Bath Town at the time, recovering from the gunshot wound to his knee. He was condemned to hang, but as he was to be executed, a vessel arrived announcing that the King had issued a proclamation prolonging the time of the Crown's pardon. Hands pleaded clemency and was pardoned. He returned to London.

Thirteen pirates, four of whom were Negro, were hanged on gibbets or trees outside Williamsburg, Virginia on Capital Landing Road (known as "Gallow's Road).

The condemned man was carried to the site in a horse-drawn cart. It halted directly beneath the gallows. He was accompanied by a minister, ordered to stand, then allowed to utter a few last words to the waiting crowd. The executioner placed the noose snugly around the neck. The cart was withdrawn.

Spectators who watched were divided as to whether the hangings were justified or not.

Governor Eden and Tobias Knight were never convicted of their relationship with Blackbeard. Spotswood reported the whole affair to the Council of trade in London. Tobias Knight was brought to trial. Israel Hands testified against him. "Tache took a present to Knight of several casks of chocolate, loaf sugar, and sweatmeats which he took from the French ships."

When asked if he knew anything about the so-called robbery of William Bell, Hands testified, "That Thache, he done robbed Mister Bell. He took money and half a barrel of brandy and a silver cup. I saw these things being loaded aboard. He said he had bought them up river. But when I heard Mister Bell describe what the robber done took, I knew it were his property."

The four pirates who accompanied Blackbeard the night he robbed Bell testified that Teach had taken Knight some presents that night. Then on the return voyage, he robbed a man at Chester's Landing. William Bell testified that the tip of Blackbeard's sword was in his boat and that the silver cup he owned was found among Blackbeard's possessions at his capture.

Tobias Knight so successfully defended himself before the court they declared the evidence against him to be false.

Governor Eden remained in office and died of yellow fever three years later. Doubt has arisen about Governor Eden's connection to Blackbeard. Some historians maintain Governor Eden was innocent of collaborating with Blackbeard.

The fight over who was to receive the reward money from the Virginia Legislature went on for four years. Those remaining in Virginia on the war ships maintained that they were entitled to their share, but those taking part in the conflict, believed that since they were the ones who fought and actually killed and captured the pirates, only they should be rewarded.

Eventually it was decided no reward was earned for Blackbeard or the others who had not been taken alive. The remaining reward was divided. Those in combat received a larger share than those remaining in Virginia. Maynard received two combat shares.

The invasion of North Carolina by Virginia caused quite a dispute between the two colonies. Governor Eden was angered that Maynard had stolen the goods belonging to him and he lodged a protest to Governor Spotswood. He claimed Governor Spotswood had no legal right to invade North Carolina waters and insisted that the captured pirates be returned to North Carolina for trial. This was odd because he made no such plea to Governor Johnson from South Carolina when Stede Bonnet had been taken from Cape Fear. In this case, the South Carolinian forces illegally entered North Carolina waters, and no one objected.

Places such as Blunt's Creek near Washington, Holliday's Island near Edenton, Ocracoke, Hog island, Cedar Island, Beaufort, Bath, and as far north as New Jersey and as far south as Georgia have been dug up looking for Blackbeard's loot. A few old coins, possibly from that era, have been found, but people are still searching.

The death of Blackbeard brought to an end the age of piracy along the North Carolina coast. On occasions after this, pirates came, but they were quickly repelled. Never again did pirates attempt to make a base of operations on The Outer Banks.

It is said that Blackbeard's skull was fashioned into a silver plated drinking bowl to be used for alcoholic beverages, of course.

If this is so, Blackbeard is probably grinning about it, wherever he is.

"BLACKBEARD SLEPT HERE"

Each generation has added to the legend of Blackbeard until there are almost as many houses and islands haunted by stories of him and his treasure as there are houses and inns where George Washington slept.

When a pirate buried treasure, did you know it was supposed to be accompanied by a prisoner to guard it? If Blackbeard buried one of his crew at each hiding place, it would explain what happened to his missing crew members.

Rumors of Blackbeard's treasure are scattered from New Hampshire to Georgia.

After a trip to England, Blackbeard brought a beautiful young woman back with him to Smutty Nose Island, New Hampshire. While he was burying his treasure, the woman explored the island. A British man-of-war surprised him before they got back together. He sailed off, leaving her there alone. She waited in vain the remainder of her life for his return. For over 100 years, her ghost has been seen flitting about the island still looking for her lost lover.

At McIntosh, Georgia, there is an island named "Blackbeard's Island" where he also buried treasure. The island is now a refuge for birds.

Many years after the battle at Teach's Hole at Ocracoke Inlet, an old Portuguese sailor, who claimed he was once a member of Blackbeard's crew, was positive Blackbeard buried his treasure at Mulberry Island, York River in Virginia.

Many places in North Carolina claim an association with Blackbeard.

At the water's edge on a farm near Oriental, between the Neuse River and the Smith and Gree Creeks, Blackbeard rested between voyages. He posted a sentinel in the branches of an ancient tree called "Teach's Oak." Although the area has been dug up in search of treasure, none was ever found.

Holliday's Island in the Chowan River is another of his chosen spots.

Since the territory along the rivers emptying into the Albemarle Sound was the older, more densely populated portion of the colony, Blackbeard visited there many times. A few miles south of Elizabeth City is a "quaint old two-story house" known as "the old Brick House." At the foot of the front steps is a small circular slab of stone, possibly an old corn grinding stone with the inscription, "E. T. – 1709," raising the suggestion it was connected to Blackbeard. The house is mainly wood with sides of brick and stone. It has a secret panel which can be opened to gain access to the basement below into a tunnel leading to the banks of the river. Blackbeard used this tunnel to escape when the law was after him. This is interesting but whoever started the story should have studied his history more carefully since the date is wrong if the grinding stone was intended to connect it to Edward Teach. The earliest date Blackbeard could possibly have been in North Carolina was 1717. According to descendants of the original owner, the house was not built until 1735.

A black farmer, Dallas Gordon, in 1938, on a farm about 15 miles east of Bath, near the mouth of the Pamlico River, was plowing his field when he dug up two or three ingots of melted gold. He had purchased the farm for about $500.

Near Wilmington, there lies a small island of several acres called "Money Island." It is called this because this is where Captain William Kidd buried a large part of his loot. But some also connect it to Blackbeard.

Judge Whedbee says that Blackbeard had a sister he used to visit on a farm near the present town of Grimesland in Pitt County. Her name was Susie Whitefield. This indicates that Blackbeard remained in touch with his family in England after he became a pirate. When he was recovering from wounds he received in battle, or just to rest between trips, his sister welcomed him at Grimes Plantation. He posted a lookout in a tall cypress tree on the banks of the Tar River.

Another tree connected to Blackbeard was located near the mouth of the Cape Fear River in Brunswick County. Family traditions says the tree has been called "Blackbeard's Tree" as far back as 1840 but little else is remembered about it.

Blackbeard still haunts not only Ocracoke Inlet where he was killed, but wanders up and down the coast of North Carolina searching for his lost head. Apparently he does not want to meet his cohort, the Devil or his former cronies, without his head, lest he would not be recognized. When storms come and strong winds blow loose sand as bullets against window panes, his spirit rises searching hither and yon for his lost head. Weird sounds are heard almost like him groaning,

"Whe-r-re is my head?" Footsteps of his mighty boots stomping up the steps or tramping on the deck of a ship echo across the land, searching, ever searching . . .

Sometimes the apparition carries a lantern to better locate likely hiding places. Any unanswered light observed along the coast is explained by calling it "Teach's light." It has been seen on board ships, in the water, in houses, and along sandy shores. The shadow of his body is observed below the surface of the water at Teach's Hole, swimming round and round, still searching for his severed head.

MEMBERS OF BLACKBEARD'S CREW

It would be interesting to see a complete list of all the men who sailed with Blackbeard, but of course this is impossible. In the "Queen Anne's Revenge," he began with 300 men. When he had the combined crews of Bonnet and Harriot, he commanded approximately 400 men.

The final battle at Ocracoke Inlet began with only Blackbeard and 18 other men. Six more were arrested later at Bath Town.

Those listed as killed in the battle with Maynard were: Joseph Brooks Sr, Joseph Curtice, Garrat Gibbons, John Husk, Nathaniel Jackson, Thomas Miller, John Martin, and Owen Roberts.

Those hanged at Williamsburg, Virginia, were: James Blake, Joseph Brooks Jr, John Carnes, Ceasar, Stephen Daniel, Thomas Gates, John Gills, Richard Greensail, John Martin, Joseph Phillips, James Robbins, Edward Salter, Richard Stiles, and James White.

What happened to the others?

John Rose Archer, who served in Blackbeard's crew, became an honest fishermen, then turned pirate again.

Israel Hands was a navigator, then commanded of one of Blackbeard's vessels. He was not present at the final battle, but was captured at Bath Town, found guilty, then released. He was last seen limping around London, begging.

Samuel Odell was taken from a trading vessel the day before the battle, received 70 wounds, recovered, was tried and then acquitted.

Lieutenant Richards, who was second-in-command to Blackbeard was not present at the battle.

William Cunningham, a one-time gunner for Blackbeard, was hanged December 12, 1718 by Governor Rogers at New Providence.

When he wrecked the "Queen Anne's Revenge" at Old Topsail Inlet, Blackbeard deserted 17 men on a desolate sandbar opposite Beaufort. He took with him only the men he found "trustworthy" and necessary to operate the "Adventure," a smaller vessel. Some remained in the area. Others joined other pirate ships.

After the battle at Ocracoke, the survivors told a tale of an extra crew member. It seems that there was one more crew member than there was supposed to be. Sometimes he was seen on the deck and sometimes he was seen below deck. No one knew who he was or where he came from. Then as suddenly as he had appeared, he disappeared. The crew members insisted the extra man was Blackbeard's co-hort, the Devil himself.

What happened to the other survivors?

Some no doubt joined other pirate crews, eventually dangling from a hangman's noose. Others attempted to pick up their lives where they had left off. This was not easy. It was like they had returned from a war. After experiencing the excitement of danger and killing, it was difficult to adjust to the humdrum existence of their pre-pirate days, so they resorted to thievery.

GOOD NEWS!

On March 3, 1997 at a news conference, North Carolina state archaeologists and a private research company announced the discovery of a sunken ship off Beaufort. They believe it to be Blackbeard's flagship the "Queen Anne's Revenge."

This caused ripples of excitement and a renewed interest in the pirate Blackbeard all over the world.

Representatives of Intersal Inc, a Boca Raton, Florida research company claim responsibility for the find. Divers have already salvaged a 288-year-old bronze bell, the brass barrel of a blunderbuss, a cannonball and other items.

The ship is lying in about 20 feet of murky water in an area called the "Graveyard of the Atlantic," less than two miles off shore, within sight of Fort Macon.

Local folks have always known that Blackbeard's ship was lost in this general area. It was a favorite fishing spot. Bob Simpson, who writes an outdoors column for the News and Observer, states: "a heap of tackle, including mine, has been lost over that wreck." He adds with a touch of humor, "Now they're going to

make it out of bounds, and probably won't even
give us back our fishhooks."

As is stated earlier in this book, Blackbeard
deliberately ran the ship aground in June of
1718.

Newspaper accounts refer to the Blackbeard
book written by Robert E. Lee, BLACKBEARD THE
PIRATE, which claims that both the ships, the
"Queen Anne's Revenge" and the "Adventure"
appeared to be wrecked beyond repair. However
after this, Lee states that Blackbeard, in the
"Adventure," applied for and received papers
to go on trading missions using the "Adventure."

Yet some authorities claim the "Adventure"
is lying on the ocean bottom next to the "Queen
Anne's Revenge."

According to the North Carolina Maritime
Museum, the Queen Anne's Revenge was built about
1710 in England. It was named the Concord and
carried 20 guns. In 1710 it was captured by
the French. They modified the ship and gave
it the French spelling, "Concorde." They believe
it was involved in slave trade.

In 1717 it was captured by pirates Hornigold
and Blackbeard. Blackbeard remodeled the vessel
for his use as a pirate ship and installed 20
more cannon. It was with this ship, Blackbeard
blockaded Charleston, South Carolina.

After he wrecked the Queen Amnne's Revenge
off Beaufort Inlet, he stole everything he
considered valuable from it and two other ships.
But this does not mean that there are no items
on board of historical value.

The first person to step foot on the sunken

ship was diver Will Kirkman from Beaufort, North Carolina. On November 19, 1996 Jeremy Davis and Will Kirkman were diving from the ship, "Pelican III." Since Davis was suffering from a sinus problem, he could not dive to the bottom. Kirkman was surprised to find that he was standing on what appeared to be a wooden floor.

At first he wasn't sure what he had. They had been diving under contract with Intersal of Florida, a salvage company primarily interested in hunting treasure. Kirkman could see what looked like a pile of logs.

He brought up a hunk of wood about five feet long, thinking scientists could discern from it the type of wood and the approximate age.

Since Intersol could see no value in a hunk of wood, it was thrown overboard.

Two days later, those involved decided that the ship probably was Blackbeard's "Queen Anne's Revenge."

When asked what made them think so, Kirkman said, "Because of its location. No other ship during that period was known to have sunk there. When Blackbeard wrecked the ship, it was off old Beaufort Inlet. Taking into account storms and shifting sands, this was the correct site."

Kirkman says the bell is about 12" to 18" tall and has the date 1709 engraved on it. At first it was believed to be silver but later was proved to be bronze. The piece of a gun was from a short blunderbuss. The pile of logs he saw were really encrusted cannon.

Kirkman said the discovery was a group effort.

It will take years to recover the artifacts
from the ship. It is doubtful if the entire
ship will be raised. Since this is considered
an archaeological find, diving archaeologists
will be involved.

If this does indeed prove to be Blackbeard's
"Queen Anne's Revenge," the greatest wealth
from the find is not expected to be gold or
silver or precious jewels, but from tourism
attracted to the city where the artifacts are
eventually displayed.

THE BALLAD OF BLACKBEARD

by Robert Day

Edward Drummond was his given name,
He came from proper stock;
An educated, wealthy mother,
And Father hard as a rock.
They wanted the best for young Edward,
But he would have no part,
Of their up-town high-brow plans:
Instead, he'd follow his heart.

He'd always wanted to go to sea,
Since he was a young lad;
He hung around the docks and wharves,
And, oh, the dreams he had!
Dreams of sailing the open seas,
Of mastering his own ship,
With a cutlass in his hand,
And a side-arm on his hip.

First, he got an education,
And then he learned the ropes,
Of being a fearsome pirate,
And fulfilling all his hopes.
He'd be the best damned pirate,
This world would ever know,
So he changed his name to Edward Teach,
And a-sailing he did go.

Now Edward was a gangly man,
'Fore long he rose to the top;
But, to be a pirate captain,
You had to handle a fearsome lot.
So he grew his beard long and shaggy,
His appearance was quite striking;
And he dealt punishment with an iron hand,
To those not of his liking.

He soon was known as Blackbeard,
"The Terror of the Seas."
He'd plunder ships of any land,
But the French were his enemies.
For they'd held him in their prison,
Like a sardine in a can;
And tho' Blackbeard was smart and wise,
He was not a forgiving man.

He raided ships both far and wide,
Off the West Indies shore.
And the Bahamas became his pot-of-call,
But he wanted much, much more.
So he traveled to the "New Land,"
And he ravaged and he pillaged,
Every ship off Carolina's coast;
'Til he landed in a small village---

A village known as Bath Town,
And there he built a home,
You'd think that he was tired of pirating,
He'd no longer roam.
But Blackbeard was a restless sort,
Not one to lay down roots,
So he kept on searching for easy prey,
To capture and to loot.

Chorus:

Now Blackbeard was the fiercest pirate,
"The Terror of the Coast."
And they say he'd bury treasure,
'Most anywhere he'd go.
And the folks in Carolina,
Know that somewhere on that beach,
There was treasure buried in the sand,
By Blackbeard, Edward Teach.

Now Blackbeard met his demise,
Near the isle of Ocracoke.
He'd fired upon an English ship,
And thought it was a joke;
But when he pulled up to its side,
To take the loot and "dough,"
He was surprised when the English crewmen,
Came up from below.

Blackbeard took a shot in the side,
From Maynard, the English captain;
But he kept on swinging his cutlass,
Oblivious to what was happening.
And when Blackbeard had him in his sights,
He received a blow to the neck;
The "Pirate King," "Terror of the Seas,"
Fell upon the deck.

After the battle was ended,
Maynard shouted to his crew,
"Cut the head off that damned pirate!
Let's show the people who we slew!"
But their welcome was not friendly,
As they sailed into Bath Town;
For Blackbeard had given their town a name,
And Maynard had shot him down.

Chorus:

Now Blackbeard was the fiercest pirate,
"The Terror of the Coast."
And they say he'd bury treasure
'Most anywhere he'd go.
And the folks in Carolina,
Know that somewhere on that beach,
There was treasure buried in the sand,
By Blackbeard, Edward Teach.

Yea, the folks in Carolina
Know that somewhere on that beach,
There's still treasure buried in the sand,
By Blackbeard, Edward Drummond,
            Edward Teach.

And Blackbeard was the greatest pirate,
The "Terror of the Coast."
And they say he'd bury treasure,
'Most anywhere he'd go.
So if you live in Carolina,
Or travel to the beach;
You just might find the treasure,
Of Blackbeard, Edward Drummond, Edward Teach.

129

BIBLIOGRAPHY

Ballance, Alton. Ocracokers, University of North
    Carolina Press, Chapel Hill, NC. 1989.

"Bath, North Carolina's First Town." NC Dept of
    Cultural Resources.

Botting Douglas & Editors of Time Life Books.
    The Pirates--The Seafarers, Alexandria VA.
    1978.

Colonial Records of NC, Vol I-X. Edited by WL
    Saunders, 1958. Raleigh, State Printer,
    1886-1890.

Davis, Maurice. The History of the Hammock House
    and Related Trivia, Beaufort, NC 1984.

de la Croix, Robert. A History of Piracy, Manor
    Books, Inc. NY, 1978.

Golden Age of Pirates. NY: Holt, Rinehart &
    Winston, 1969.

Johnson, Captain Charles. A General History of
    the Robberies and Murders of the Most Notorious
    Pirates, London, 1924.

Lee, Robert E. Blackbeard the Pirate, John F.
    Blair, Winston Salem NC, 1974.

130

Lewis, Taylor and Young, Joanne. The Hidden
Treasure of Bath Town, Friends of Historic
Bath, Inc. 1978.

Marine Research Society, The Pirates Own Book,
Dover Publications Inc, NY.

Rankin, Hugh F. The Pirates of Colonial North
Carolina, Dept. of Cultural Resources, Div.
of Archives and History, Raleigh, 1981.

Roberts, Nancy. Blackbeard and Other Pirates
of the Atlantic Coast, John F Blair, Publisher,
Winston-Salem NC 1993.

Rogorozinski, Jan. Pirates, Brigands, Buccaneers
& Privateers.

Sandbeck, Peter B. "The Historic Architecture
of New Bern and Craven County." The Tryon
Palace Commision, New Bern, NC.

Stick, David. The Outer Banks of North Carolina,
University of North Carolina Press, Chapel
Hill NC, 1958.

Walser, Richard. North Carolina Legends, NC Dept
of Cultural Resources, Div. of Archives and
History, 1982.

Whedbee, Charles Harry. Legends of the Outer
Banks, John Blair, Winston-Salem, 1966.

"Carteret County News Times," Morehead City, NC, March 1997.

"News & Observer," Raleigh, NC, March, 1997.

"Sun Journal," New Bern, NC, March 1997.